NURSE AGAINST THE TOWN

Why did the people of Barfield avoid their hospital? Why did they whisper 'criminal' about its director, Dr. Jerry Sterling, when they talked of the mysterious death of his beautiful wife, Naomi, and why did Naomi's brother seem so determined to ruin Dr. Sterling? Pretty Ellen Whitaker desperately struggled to find the answers — torn between her consuming love for Jerry and the terrible doubts that racked her own mind.

JANE CONVERSE

NURSE AGAINST THE TOWN

Complete and Unabridged

LINFORD
Leicester

First published in Great Britain

First Linford Edition
published October 1993

British Library CIP Data

Converse, Jane
Nurse against the town.—Large print ed.—
Linford romance library
I. Title II. Series
813.54 [F]

ISBN 0–7089–7456–2

Published by
F. A. Thorpe (Publishing) Ltd.
Anstey, Leicestershire

Set by Words & Graphics Ltd.
Anstey, Leicestershire
Printed and bound in Great Britain by
T. J. Press (Padstow) Ltd., Padstow, Cornwall

This book is printed on acid-free paper

1

"OH, Barfield's changed all right," Ellen Whitaker's mother agreed. "I kept writing to tell you that." There was an accusing sharpness in her tone as she said, "Chicago's far away, but it's not as though you couldn't have come home in all these years to see for yourself."

Ellen ignored the faint note of bitterness in her mother's voice, knowing it was justified, and knowing, too, that it would be erased in the next sentence. Marjorie Whitaker had never devoted more than a second or two to displaying her emotions.

Twenty years ago, when Ellen was only six and David was still an infant, the icy winds that swept over Barfield in the winter had taken Les Whitaker with them, a victim of pneumonia. It would be different today, Ellen

1

thought; at worst, her father would miss a few weeks' work with the mine engineering firm that employed him. Barfield had a hospital now. One of the faster growing, most prosperous communities in Colorado, Barfield no longer depended solely on its copper mines. Change everywhere; progress and change.

Her mother had wasted no time in feeling sorry for herself twenty years ago. The lower half of the stately old frame house had been turned into Mom Whitaker's Tea Room; room enough upstairs to make living quarters for a widow and two small children. The tea room didn't flourish, but it kept the family together. Mom's devotion to her kids had been expressed in the baking of uncounted pies, the frying of unnumbered chickens when 'tea' was expanded to the serving of Sunday dinners.

It seemed strange to be sitting with Mom and David in one of the small private dining rooms *upstairs* now, served by one of a half-dozen waitresses who worked at the now-expanded and well-patronised Whitaker Dinner House. Stranger still, after the long absence, to be sitting beside two people who reflected the same rather wistful look Ellen saw in the mirror each morning, a shy expression that seemed to be built into the finely chiselled features. The same chestnut coloured hair (though Mom's was streaked with grey and David's, close cropped, tended to curl in this damp late-April weather), and the same wide hazel eyes. Ellen's only inheritance from her father, she had been told, was a temper that flared whenever her sense of justice was outraged. Physically, she could look at her mother now and visualise herself at forty-five.

" . . . two whole new subdivisions," David was saying. "I guess you saw the new shopping district on your way from the train station."

Ellen snapped out of her introspection. "I passed a whole section of big new buildings just outside of town, too. What are . . . "

"Factories," David said. He seemed to have a personal pride in Barfield's phenomenal growth. "One's a chemical fertiliser outfit and there's the new paper mill, a clay products manufacturer and the Barfield Wood pulp Company . . . Henry Barfield's brought all kinds of new industry into town."

"Invested in a lot of it, too," Mom pointed out. "The only big thing he doesn't have his fingers in is the uranium mine. That's big business . . . belongs to some huge outside corporation."

"He's never got his hands on the original copper mine, either," David added. "He keeps trying though. It's all tied up in litigation. Profits frozen until the court decides whether it belongs to him or to Dr. Sterling."

Ellen's breath caught in her lungs at the mention of Jerry Sterling's name, but she managed to keep her voice casual. "Yes, I . . . remember Mom

4

wrote and said Henry was contesting his father's will."

"He was mad enough about most of the fortune going to his niece. But, then, after Naomi was killed — "

"Let's not dig that up again," David interrupted. "We were talking about groovy things. Like getting a junior college built here just in time for you-know-who."

"At least *one* of my children won't be leaving me for years at a time to go to college," Mom said. She took the sarcastic edge from her tone in the next breath. "Of course, you *had* to go to Chicago, dear. Considering that's where you got your scholarship."

David laughed. "Yeah, and considering Barfield didn't even have a junior college then. Or the hospital. You haven't seen that yet, Ellen."

"Tomorrow," Ellen said. She felt herself skating on thin conversational ice again. Next thing she knew, Mom and David would be asking why she had decided to come back to Barfield, to apply for a job that couldn't possibly offer the salary or career opportunities that had been hers at the Chicago hospital . . . why, when her mother and brother certainly weren't dependent on her in any way, she would return to this growing but comparatively small town where her chances of finding love were slimmer than they had been in the big city.

It would be impossible to tell them that the job, the salary, the chances for advancement were meaningless. Or that the only reason she hadn't responded to the many opportunities for romance in Chicago was right here in Barfield. A widower now, probably scarred by the shoddy death of his beautiful young wife and the ugly accusations that had followed the tragedy, Jerry Sterling would be as unaware of Ellen's love for him as he had been when, as Senior Class President and undisputed scholastic leader at Barfield High, he had barely known of a shy, chestnut-haired freshman's existence. Neither he, nor anyone else, knew that his decision to become a doctor had spurred Ellen's desire to become a nurse.

Nor did anyone know the secret agonies that had accompanied Jerry Sterling's marriage to the lovely girl whose grandfather had mined the first copper ore in this area, founding a town that still bore his name

The heartbreak was not lessened, less than a year later, when Naomi Barfield Sterling's battered body had been found in a roadside ditch twelve miles from the town. Ellen had shared Jerry's misery; again at a distance, just as she had pitied the young doctor when gossipy letters from home reported that the marriage was a stormy one.

Ellen had let another year go by before she was able to think, without suffering pangs of guilt. He's alone now. He's free. This time, working for him, seeing him every day . . . maybe he'll know I'm alive.

"Ellen? Hey, are you with us?" David was addressing her, grinning at what was probably a faraway expression.

"Sorry. I was . . . thinking."

"If it's about getting a job at the hospital," Mom said, "you needn't worry. It's such a depressing place, the turnover in nurses is shocking. But, then, they don't need a big staff."

Ellen toyed with her dessert; green apple pie made from Mom's recipe, but put together by a hired pastry-cook. "The only hospital in a boom town? Why wouldn't they need a good-sized staff?"

"For the same reason that it's depressing," David said. "Most of the beds are empty."

"Well, great. Maybe it's the spring water and the mountain air." Ellen smiled. "If old man Barfield had known this was such a healthy burg, maybe he'd have left all that money for a museum, or something." The smile faded into a puzzled frown. Just looking at David and her mother told her the facetious remark hadn't amused them. Lamely, she offered, "People around here still have babies, don't they?"

"Usually they have them in Templeton," Mom said. "Where they go for operations and . . . everything else that brings people to hospital."

"But, why? Why would they go to a hospital thirty miles away when there's a new one right here in town?"

Mom drained her coffee cup and got up from her chair. "David will tell you. And you'll find out for yourself dear. Look, I'm going to have to get downstairs. Porter Hubbard's coming in to arrange for the Men's Club Demotion Dinner. He's a busy man — I don't want to keep him waiting." She was halfway across the small private dining room when she spun around. "You remember Porter Hubbard, don't you, honey?"

Ellen nodded. "Sure."

"Come down after a bit and say hello. I know he'd love to see you." Mom paused for a moment, as if making a proud survey of the recently decorated room, no doubt pleased by the surprisingly pleasant blend of Western Rustic, Bavarian *Bierstube* and Cozy Gingerbread décors. Then she stepped out of sight, disappearing into another dining area that had once been the nursery.

David waited until he heard his mother's businesslike tread on the staircase before he turned to Ellen. "Porter's a cool guy. You ought to let him know you're back in town."

"Let's let him finish his club business first," Ellen said. "You were going to tell me why the hospital . . . "

"You're not dense," David said irritably. "Why would I have to tell you what's going on?"

"Because I don't know," Ellen told him. "You act as though . . . you and Mom both . . . as though you're avoiding the subject."

David made a wry face. "Yah. Well, in this town — especially if you're in business — you try to avoid it. In fact, you don't do what I did last year. Did Mom write you I got my shoulder dislocated? Skiing?"

"Yes."

"So I got Dr. Sterling to fix me up. Nearly cost Mom the Businessmen's Association deal. They have a luncheon meeting here every Tuesday."

"That doesn't make sense," Ellen protested.

"It does to Henry Barfield. Hey, you really don't know what goes on, do you? What do I do, start from the beginning?"

Ellen released a long breath. "Maybe you'd better."

"Well, you remember Naomi? She was in my class — I think you knew her."

"I always thought I'd be in my glory if I looked like her," Ellen recalled. "That fresh peaches-and-cream complexion and I remember how I envied her that golden blonde hair. She was beautiful, wasn't she?"

David agreed. "Not only that, but she had a lot going for her. I mean, everything that money could buy. The way she dressed, for one thing."

"She always looked like a fashion model," Ellen said.

"Sure. In fact, after she got out of high school she had a whirl at modelling in New York. Not because she needed a job — her grandfather gave her anything she wanted. Oh, and she went to some drama school, too, in California. I guess they expected her to study — you know, to really work instead of just partying around, looking terrific. So she flunked out, but I don't think she ever got over the idea of being a movie star — somebody glamorous and famous."

"But she came back here," Ellen said.

"Yah. To be with her grandfather. That's what she told everybody . . . always talking about how much she loved the old guy. I guess she knew how much he hated his son."

"Her Uncle Henry."

"Uh-huh. Naomi's father had been the old man's favourite, I guess. Then, when Naomi's folks were . . . I don't remember exactly what the accident was . . . "

"They were drowned, Mom told me once." Ellen checked her watch, wondering how far back in Barfield history David had to go before he explained Jerry Sterling's problem with the new Barfield Hospital. "It happened during a yacht cruise on the Mediterranean."

"Big storm. That's it." David remembered. "Well, Naomi was just a little kid when it happened, and after that, her grandfather really took over. Although, I understand she used to live with him most of the time even before she lost her parents. They were always off on some long vacation in Europe or somewhere. She was her grandpa's girl from the day she was born. And I hear her Uncle Henry resented the whole bit. Like, maybe he was thinking about his father's money, and who was going to get it — way back then."

"I gather he didn't get it," Ellen said.

"Nope. Just some real estate. Tokens compared to what Naomi got. But what really got him was . . . this happened while the old man was still alive . . . when Naomi fell in love with Dr. Sterling."

"What difference would that have made to him?" Ellen asked.

"Well, here's this handsome young doctor, just completed his residency. He comes back to Barfield, right? Naomi's pretty bored with the whole scene here, after New York and Hollywood." David paused, staring into the dregs of his coffee. "So she flips over Dr. Sterling, and her grandpa makes *him* the fair-haired boy. Who do you think talked the old man into shelling out the money to build the hospital? Jerry Sterling. Probably a half-million bucks right there that Henry Barfield wasn't ever going to see. But he couldn't kick up a fuss *then*."

"I suppose he did after his father died," Ellen guessed.

"Not as bad as after Naomi was

killed. You probably got all the newspaper clippings from Mom. About the inquest and all."

"Yes." Ellen swallowed down a hard lump in her throat. David was plainly reluctant to recount the details. Certainly he would find it difficult to discuss the shoddier aspects of the tragedy. Naomi's body had evidently been thrown into the roadside ditch from a car. But her death had been caused by an illegal operation. 'Criminal Butchery,' the County Medical Examiner had called it. And a poisonous finger of suspicion had pointed at Naomi's husband.

"At first, it was just gossip," David said. "You know. People remembering the Sterlings weren't getting along too well."

"I never believed that. It depressed me, but . . . I couldn't quite accept it." Ellen spoke with genuine regret; she had always visualised Jerry deliriously in love with his beautiful young wife, and she told David as much.

15

"Oh, I guess Dr. Sterling was crazy about her, all right. He really broke up after it happened." David shrugged his shoulders. "I don't know. People said she was mad because her husband spent too much time at the hospital. A girl I know used to work there as a nurse's aid . . . she said Naomi charged into the doctor's office a couple of times and made a big scene. She was bored, I guess. Maybe . . . well, some people said maybe the operation was her idea because she didn't want to be tied down to a family. And that she talked her husband into it, but then he botched the job and . . . "

"That's the most insane, the most vicious . . . "

David held up his hand to quell the tide of anger that had risen in Ellen. "I'm just telling you what some people thought."

"Hateful gossips," Ellen cried. "He wasn't accused of murder, was he? In the eyes of the law . . . ?"

"He had an airtight alibi," David

said. "He was at the hospital at the time the coroner figured that . . . " David's face coloured, adding to his uneasy appearance. " . . . that everything happened. He was completely cleared."

"That should have shut up the — "

"It shut them up," David interrupted. "But just because people stop talking about a thing doesn't mean they've stopped thinking a certain way."

"They can't still suspect that Jerry had anything to do with his wife's death!"

David released a weary sigh. "Can't they? The sheriff's office hasn't turned up a single clue."

"That makes the doctor automatically guilty?" Ellen found it difficult to control her resentment. "I suppose the people who saw Jerry at the hospital were mistaken? Or liars? Or he bribed them?"

"Or the coroner was wrong about the time of death," David added. "That's the prevailing theory."

"But a few tantrums — a few normal

spats between married people — what kind of motive would that be for murder?"

"Nobody thinks he *wanted* to kill her," David pointed out. "The way it is, it's almost worse." David fell silent for a moment. "He emerges as a bad surgeon. Understand, nobody ever comes out and says it any more. They don't even talk about the other thing . . . the reason Dr. Sterling might have . . . tried an operation like that."

"What other thing?"

David's eyes avoided Ellen's. "Well, almost everybody in town — probably everybody except Dr. Sterling — knew that Naomi ran around with other men. Even some of her old boy-friends, and she had plenty of those. Maybe when the doctor found out . . . the way he loved her, he could have just gone berserk. Or tried to avoid a scandal."

"You don't believe that, do you, David?"

Ellen's brother lifted his head to face her squarely. "That's a fine question."

18

"Answer it."

David chose his words with slow deliberation. "I don't think he's a killer, no. You know how I feel about him as a doctor; I went to him when I needed one."

"But the seed's been planted in your head, too." Ellen shook her head, more disgusted now than incensed. "So Jerry's never going to be accused, but he's always going to live under suspicion. Great! Wonderful people in my home town."

"Wait a minute! He has people loyal to him. Us, for instance. I could name others . . . "

"You mean they're few enough that you can remember their names?"

David ignored the accusation. "Among the oldtimers, sure. I've lived here all my life."

"And the new people?"

There was another brief silence before David spoke. "Most of them bought their homes in Henry Barfield's development. Or through his real estate

19

office. He's Barfield to them — not just the name — the town. Head of the Businessmen's Association, member of the Hospital Board, active in all the civic clubs. Most of the new residents owe their jobs to him. See, Henry Barfield didn't inherit much, but he sure parlayed what he *did* get into a big pile. As Mom says, it became sort of an obsession with him. Money and power. That, and . . . wrecking Dr. Sterling."

Ellen had been listening to the last few sentences in complete bewilderment. "Dave — did you say Henry Barfield's on the *Hospital Board*?"

"Oh, sure. It's an elective office. The hospital belongs to the city, and . . . "

"Then you've got to be wrong," Ellen insisted. "A man doesn't sit on a hospital board and try to destroy the doctor in charge. That's like trying to destroy the hospital."

"Don't ask me," David said. "I only know there's no love lost between Mr. Barfield and the doctor. And *Mrs.*

Barfield — she's not even as subtle as Henry. It's a miracle they haven't poisoned Lorna."

Ellen frowned. "Lorna? Oh, I remember . . . "

"Their daughter. She's a freshman at the college. I see her quite a lot." In response to Ellen's quizzical glance, David assured her quickly that the relationship was a casual one. "I've got a girl I want you to meet, but she's not one of the Barfield clan. Joan and her folks are part of the pro-Sterling camp."

"The minority," Ellen said. She felt a sudden bitterness towards the whole community. An hour ago she had been looking forward to strolling down the tree-lined streets, greeting old acquaintances, drinking in the familiar sights and enjoying the discovery of new shops, new homes, new faces. Now she half regretted her return to a town where everyone you met had to be classified as pro- or anti-Jerry Sterling. "You'll have to keep me

21

posted, Dave," she said. "Give me a scorecard, so I'll know the good guys from the bad guys."

"They're all good people," her brother protested. He was on his feet now, obviously relieved that the discussion was nearing its end, and evidently anxious to keep an appointment he had mentioned earlier. "Nobody's really sure of what happened. You can't blame a person if he thinks . . . "

"I'll decide for myself whether I blame them or not," Ellen said. She was surprised by the edginess in her voice. "Just let me know who's who."

"You'll get better information downstairs," David was on his way out of the room.

"From Mom?"

"Porter Hubbard."

Ellen followed her brother to the stairwell. "Where does he stand?"

"For one thing, he's president of the Hospital Board," David said. "For another, he's the one person in this town who's stood behind the doc, one hundred per cent. If Hubbard wasn't so popular, and Dr. Sterling didn't have him for a friend, the doc would have been run out of town months ago."

Ellen followed her brother down the stairs, suddenly interested in reviving an acquaintance that had meant nothing to her a few seconds before. Even David had disappointed her. It would be good to shake the hand of the one person in Barfield, besides herself, who believed in Jerry Sterling without reservations.

Yet, as she crossed the main dining room, walking towards the partitioned cubicle that served as her mother's office, a disturbing thought gnawed at her. What did she know about Jerry? How could she say she knew him; truly knew him, swearing to his competence as a doctor, firmly believing in his innocence, defending him as a man whose reputation was being shattered by innuendo and not by evidence? She loved a stranger. Even people you knew well changed with the years. What if . . .

The thought frightened her, but the intensity of her love remained unchanged. Ellen almost ran the last few steps to the office door, eager for reassurance from a man who knew Jerry Sterling, had been his best friend since childhood, and remained his best friend now.

2

ELLEN remembered Porter Hubbard as Barfield High's star halfback, and the years had done little to change his football-player image. No one who didn't know him would have suspected him of being an accountant — a tax expert with a prosperous career as a business consultant.

Porter was built along massive lines, and his hearty laugh and personality added to the general effect of expansiveness. Ellen could visualise him using those big hands to pat backs, pump warm and energetic handshakes, winning over enemies in the town's political controversies and gaining friends with consummate ease.

Not the least of Porter Hubbard's attractions was a ready smile and an expression of complete honesty and interest. Interest. Yes, that was it, Ellen decided. He looked at you as though you were someone terribly important, and he listened to you as though every word you uttered was of monumental significance.

"Porter's our village greeter," Mom said shortly after he had welcomed Ellen back to town. "He's a one-man Chamber of Commerce. Listen to him, you'd think Barfield was Eden, Shangri-La and the outer fringes of heaven, all rolled into one."

Porter laughed his appreciation, squeezing Mom's shoulder affectionately. "It is, it is! Some of us never did tear ourselves away. And then you have the prodigals like Ellen, here."

A waitress appeared at the door, reporting some minor matter that demanded Mrs. Whitaker's attention. It seemed to Ellen that her mother seized the opportunity to leave the room with undisguised eagerness. She excused herself, encouraging Porter to make himself at home, and tossing a pleased half-smile in Ellen's direction.

Ellen seated herself in her mother's desk chair. Porter pulled up a spindly maple settee closer to the desk, lowering his huge frame into it gingerly. "I can't tell you how happy I am to see you back. Your mother indicated you're here for keeps. Is that right?"

"I don't know," Ellen said. "A . . . a lot will depend on the job situation."

Porter had started a leisurely process of lighting his pipe. Now he waved the match back and forth carelessly, extinguishing it as he spoke. "That shouldn't be a problem. I handle the accounts for any number of firms that can use a sharp secretary."

Ellen frowned. "I'm an R.N., Porter. I don't want an office job."

He made a self-deprecating gesture. "What's wrong with me? I forgot. Well, that's no problem, either, dear. Show me a hospital in the country that can't use one more good nurse."

"My brother says you're president of the Hospital Board," Ellen said.

Porter laughed again; laughter came easily to him, lighting up the naturally affable expression. "I get all the presidencies that are left over — the ones Henry Barfield can't find time for."

"I would think he'd find time for *that* one," Ellen said pointedly.

For an instant, Porter's eyes clouded with a dark seriousness, almost a wariness. Then, flashing his broad happy football-player's grin again, he said. "You've been hearing."

"I've been hearing," Ellen echoed. "From what I've gathered, you're about the only real friend Jerry Sterling has in this town."

"You've been hearing wrong," Porter said. His deep voice was softened by a kind understanding. "We have our misunderstandings, Ellen. Any city that's experiencing rapid change — fast growth and progress — is going to require decisions, but I say let bygones be bygones. We have a job to do in this town. Working together." He stopped abruptly, probably sensing that Ellen would demand a more direct statement. Turning towards her, he said, "Look, I'm not going to deny that there's some friction. The courts will settle the financial aspect . . ."

"And the pressure?" Ellen asked. "The gossip and the pressure to . . ."

"To replace Jerry? That will pass, too," Porter insisted. "My policy is to avoid widening the chasm. I'm solidly behind Jerry, and Henry Barfield knows it."

"But you don't want to buck him head-on," Ellen guessed. She beat Porter to mouthing the next triteness. "You can win more flies with honey than with vinegar."

"That's it exactly," Porter cried. The sarcasm eluded him completely. "Exactly. I try to see Henry's viewpoint and I try to make him see Jerry in proper perspective. Anything short of a compromise wouldn't help either of them."

"How can you compromise with

injustice?" Ellen asked.

Porter's reply was quick and direct. "By changing a man's idea of what's just. You weren't here, Ellen. Remember, it's been a trying ordeal for Henry and for Carrie. Why, I was willed a more valuable piece of property than the old Mr. Barfield left to his own son. Just because I handled his books for years and took time to play chess with the old codger. It took me a long time to get Henry and his wife to stop resenting me for that."

"But you did?"

"I'm happy to say that we're on the best of terms today. And that's not disloyalty to Jerry, believe me. I'm close enough to the Barfields to . . . to be able to influence them. Soften their views, make them see that the town needs the hospital and the hospital needs Jerry. Isn't that more constructive than taking a belligerent position, tearing the town wider apart? Wait and see, Ellen." Porter puffed on his pipe, probably recalling with satisfaction other, lesser conflicts he had resolved with his ability to see both viewpoints. He steered the conversation into a related but less aggravating channel. "Have you seen the hospital?"

Ellen shook her head. "No. I thought I'd get David to drive me over in the morning."

"Are you busy now?"

"No, but I . . . " Ellen shot an involuntary glance towards the rust-coloured knit suit she had travelled in. "I'm not very presentable."

"You look fine to me," Porter assured her. "I'm free this evening. Suppose we run over there now? Really, I'm anxious to get your opinion. We're all very proud of our facilities, of course, but a big-city nurse might not be as impressed." Porter was urging Ellen out of her chair, enthusiastic and insistent. "Come along."

Ellen got to her feet reluctantly. Apart from her rumpled suit, there was her plan to wash and set her hair this evening, to walk into Jerry's office looking fresh and . . .

"We won't see anyone important, if you're being silly enough to think you don't look beautiful." Porter had linked his arm through Ellen's, guiding her out of the small room. "At this hour, there won't be but one nurse on duty. Dr. Vosbergh won't be there, I'm sure."

Crossing the main dining room, a sudden panic stifled Ellen's breath. "We don't have to see Jerry — Dr. Sterling, do we? I have my references at the house, and . . . "

"You don't even have to talk to him about the job until tomorrow, if that's the way you'd like it," Porter said. "Not that he'll notice how you look. Jerry's got eyes for his work and nothing else. Anyway, there's no question that you'll be hired."

Ellen decided to ignore the disappointing remark about Jerry. "Only one nurse on the three-to-eleven shift. I should think you *do* need nurses!"

"Well we're . . . not *that* busy," Porter admitted. "Not too many patients right now."

To this confusion, and to Ellen's inner tumult, her mother added a final bewilderment about the Barfield Hospital. Told that Porter was going to give her daughter 'The fifty-cent guided tour', Mom said, "That's awfully sweet of you, Porter, but can you spare the time?"

"For a pretty girl? A lonely bachelor? What a question, Mrs. Whitaker." Porter beamed at Ellen's mother as though she were the pretty girl under discussion. "I think we're all squared away on the Demotion Dinner, aren't we? So — I'm a free agent. I'm going to show Ellen the hospital and, if she likes, some of our wild night life."

Mom's approving expression was almost embarrassing. "I was just thinking, this is choir practice night at the church. You never miss that." To Ellen, she said, "Porter has the most marvellous bass voice. You'll have to hear him Sunday."

"Don't drive her out of town, Mother — we just got her back." Porter chuckled, then explained, "Mrs. Agnew's out of town. Left this morning. Can't have practice without our accompanist, so the Reverend phoned today and called it off."

Ellen had a fleeting moment to wonder where the minister's wife, who was also the church organist, had gone alone and on such short notice. Mom answered the unspoken question. "Oh, come to think of it, someone *did* tell me Mrs. Agnew went to Templeton. Had an attack last night. Well, I kept telling her, a suspected gall stone condition is nothing to fool with. But the Reverend's so busy, and she hated the thought of going in for all those nasty tests, lying there all alone with practically no visitors. How long will she be gone, Porter?"

"Just a few days," Porter said. "Unless they decide to operate. The Reverend seems to think they will."

Mom clicked her tongue in sympathy, and suddenly the staggering implications of the conversation struck Ellen with the impact of a body blow. The minister's wife, one of the people who set examples for Barfield, had postponed medical care because going into hospital in another town was inconvenient. But she had gone! And here was Mom, one of Barfield's successful business people, discussing the matter with the president of the Hospital Board as though it were standard procedure. As though it was perfectly natural to avoid the doctor who had convinced Old Man Barfield that a hospital was desperately needed *here*!

Nor did it help to note, when Porter Hubbard pulled his new Lincoln into the parking area outside the small but gleamingly new hospital, that the building had been erected on a half-acre directly across the street from the church. Even more chilling was Ellen's recollection of the minister and his wife.

Kindly people. Understanding people. Never vindictive, never unjust. They were foremost among the 'good people' David had lauded, and Jerry Sterling had probably eaten his boyhood fill at ice-cream sociables on that lawn across the street.

How could you condemn people for turning their backs on a man you were about to face for the first time in ten years?

Porter was guiding her along a hedge-lined sidewalk towards glass double doors. "What do you think of the outside? Beautiful, isn't it?"

"Beautiful," Ellen agreed. Her legs had started to tremble and it was almost impossible to fill her lungs with air.

3

ELLEN'S mind had posed the awesome questions about Jerry Sterling's innocence. Her heart answered them.

She still hoped to avoid a meeting with Jerry this evening, less concerned now with her appearance than with her shaking emotions. Porter Hubbard, however, saw no reason for passing Jerry's office without stopping in.

They were headed in that direction, walking the immaculate and spacious corridors of the single-storeyed hospital. Porter pointing out the surgical suite, the nursery, the attractively decorated rooms. Compared with the city-within-a-city where Ellen had worked in Chicago, Barfield Hospital looked more like an extended medical suite. Still its décor was cheerful and, more important, it was well equipped. Porter had reason to show it off proudly. What he avoided comment on, and what sent a queasy chill through Ellen's insides, was the almost total absence of patients.

It was like a ghost town — the nursery dark, the tiny bassinets empty. Doors yawned open in the wards, revealing unoccupied beds. A lone nurse bobbed her head in greeting as Ellen and Porter passed a nurses' station; otherwise, they encountered no personnel. Inconceivable, Ellen thought. A growing town should be raising funds to extend its hospital; this one should have been just barely large enough to provide for a town the size of Barfield. Instead, it was nearly deserted.

Citizens avoiding a hospital that belonged to them! It made no sense! If people really believed the worst about Jerry, why didn't they demand his expulsion? Why this polite, hypocritical boycott? Why these empty rooms, and this deadly silence? Other questions assailed Ellen; in the almost unused hospital, why would they need another nurse? If she didn't work here, how could she stay in Barfield?

One glance at Jerry Sterling and Ellen knew that she had to stay. In that tremulous instant, she knew, also, that her love for him was unchanged and genuine. It was an old love, a deep love, but it was not blind; they were strangers to each other, but Ellen believed what virtually no one in this town believed: Barfield was punishing an innocent man.

Jerry Sterling was sitting behind a large modern desk as Porter and Ellen came to the doorway. Porter's voice boomed in the hushed corridor. "Hi, Jerry. Too busy for company?"

A bright crook-necked lamp illuminated the sheaf of papers before him, and the doctor blinked as he rose to his feet, straining to see through the dim light beyond his desk. "Hullo, Porter. I was just finishing up. Come in."

"I brought a visitor," Porter said.

"So I see." The voice sounded weary

beyond belief, but there was no tremor of weakness in it.

He had not changed physically. His face was still too thin, his black hair still a trifle long and unruly. Tall, as slim as he had always been, he wore his medical jacket as though he had always worn it, looking as Ellen had imagined he would in whites. The same sensitive mouth, the same high cheekbones that testified to his one-eighth Indian ancestry; why was it, Ellen wondered, that she would not have recognised him in the street?

As Porter performed the amenities, reintroducing Jerry Sterling and Ellen with the air one assumed they would remember each other, Ellen looked directly into the dark eyes that stared at her, disappointingly, without recognition. The change, she realised, lay there; in the black depths of Jerry's eyes.

She had evidently been lost in thought, for Porter's voice startled her. He was thanking Jerry for the offer to show his guest around the hospital, saying, "We've already made the rounds, thanks. I know how busy you are, taking care of patients and doing the administrative job, too."

Jerry gestured at a pair of leather chairs facing his desk. Solemnly, he invited Ellen and Porter to sit down. "We don't often have visitors," he added.

They were settled, then, and Ellen was grateful for Porter's easy garrulousness: she felt too tense, too nervous in Jerry Sterling's presence to think of the proper things to say. Porter suffered from no such problem, though he had apparently forgotten that this was not to be Ellen's job interview. "Ellen knew more about what I was showing her than I do. She's a nurse, you know."

"I didn't know," Jerry said. "Just visiting the old home town, Miss Whitaker?"

"No, I . . . " Ellen held her breath for an instant. There was no point now in holding back her reason for coming to the hospital. "I'm planning to stay. I

41

was hoping you could use an R.N. I'm sure I can get accredited in the state." Quickly, she gave a brief description of her training and experience.

Jerry's face remained impassive, his voice quiet and businesslike. "You worked in surgery," he said. "We don't have an experienced scrub nurse here. We need one to stand by, but you'd have to do general duty most of the time." He paused, as though waiting for an objection. Then, lowering his intensely probing gaze to the desk top, he murmured, "It seems fair to tell you that my only colleague here, Dr. Vosbergh, no longer performs operations. He . . . considers himself too old to do surgery. He has a small private practice and he brings his patients here, but at the present time I'm the only doctor on the staff. And I . . . " Jerry stopped, releasing an audible sigh. "I don't often . . . "

There was an agonising silence, during which Ellen knew he was groping for a way to tell her that he had no surgical patients.

Ellen found the quiet unbearable. "I understand, Doctor. In a . . . new hospital, until it becomes an established part of the community and people start using its services, the staff has to be flexible. Isn't that what you mean?"

Jerry continued staring at the papers on his desk for a moment. Then, abruptly, he dropped a heavy hand to the desk top and looked up at Ellen. "No. No, that's not what I mean at all. There should be room here for three or four full-time surgical nurses on each shift. An equal number in OB, and six times the R.N.'s we have on general floor duty now." He turned to Porter. "I wish you'd explain the situation to Miss Whitaker. I don't want to hire anyone under false pretences."

"You've never done that," Porter argued.

Jerry's face had tightened into a grim mask. "There are some who think so. The nurse who quit yesterday came here from Denver. She didn't know the ... 'facts' until her landlady told her. I will say, though, that Miss Carstairs was very discreet in resigning." The bitterness in Jerry's tone filled the room, though he barely enunciated the words: "She didn't actually use the terms, but she made it clear that she couldn't risk working for a probable abortionist. A butcher."

Porter leaned forward in his chair. "Jerry, don't."

"I'm not dramatising myself. I'm telling the truth." Jerry got to his feet. "When you've filled Miss Whitaker in on the whole background, if she wants to work here, I'll be glad to give her one of our applications. Meanwhile, I don't want anyone else ostracised in the community. Contaminated by contact with me. The few people who work here don't seem to care about issues. They have their jobs and ... I don't delude myself that they stay out of any deep loyalty. I don't expect too much from people who work in this profession for a pay-cheque only. We *do* need better nursing care. Need it desperately."

"Dr. Sterling?" It seemed strange to be calling him that, when in Ellen's daydreams she had always called him Jerry.

He was walking Ellen and Porter to the door, indicating that the visit was over; he had work to do. Or silent brooding. "Yes?"

They had stopped in the doorway. "If salary was an object, I would have stayed in Chicago. And I'm not afraid of being ostracised."

"You don't seem to know . . . "

"I know everything you've been trying to tell me, Doctor." Ellen's earlier tremulousness was gone. It was the old Whitaker trait her mother had told her about, the fiery reaction to injustice, she had inherited from her father. Outrage, first. Then, after the anger, a drawing from some deep reservoir of strength, the old shyness replaced by a firm resolve. "May I take an application form with me?"

She was able to meet those dark, troubled eyes now; eyes that explored her own with more doubt than gratitude, as though Jerry had been hurt and rejected so many times that any show of solidarity was questioned.

He was speechless for several seconds, and then Porter Hubbard said quietly, "She asked for an application form, Jerry."

Jerry crossed the office to open the drawer of a filing cabinet. He moved slowly, like a man in a dream, and the fury with Barfield blazed once more inside Ellen. How could 'good people' do this to a man who had suffered through a heartbreaking tragedy, a man who wanted nothing more than the right he had earned; to ease the pain, to heal the sickness and wounds of the very people who crucified him?

To save him from further humiliation, and to ward off the tears that would well up in her eyes in another moment, Ellen affected a crisp, businesslike attitude.

She accepted the printed forms Jerry Sterling handed to her as though they were employment questionnaires only and not declarations of faith. "Thank you, Doctor. All right if I fill these in at home tonight and return them in the morning? Along with my references?"

Jerry was not beaten yet. They had not ground dignity from him. His steady tone matched Ellen's. "That will be fine, Miss Whitaker. We can talk about your State Board examinations then."

He shook hands with Porter, thanked Ellen for her interest, and returned to his desk. He was sitting there, a study in loneliness, his surgeon's hands illuminated by the bright desk lamp, as Porter ushered Ellen away from the door.

Nothing was said until Porter had taken his seat beside Ellen in the big Lincoln. Then Porter's fist pounded heavily against the centre of the steering wheel. "Damn them," he muttered. "They don't deserve him."

47

"The 'good people' of Barfield?" Ellen asked.

"Every time I see Jerry, it becomes harder to go on being the diplomat. I know I'll only hurt him if I come out at this town with fists flying, but . . . " Porter Hubbard shook his head back and forth, his facial muscles tense. "You don't educate people by making enemies of them. Not when they think . . . "

"Educate them," Ellen whispered. "I don't think I have that kind of self-control."

Porter turned from the wheel to face her. "Fight them? How, Ellen?"

She lowered her eyes. Throw out contempt into the faces of people who honestly believe Jerry was guilty? Lash out at them, when a short while ago she herself had been uncertain? "I suppose by . . . doing what he's doing," Ellen said. "Trying to make Barfield Hospital the best possible hospital. The only way I know how, Porter. By being a good nurse."

"Jerry was trying to tell you, back there, that the job's going to make greater demands on you than that."

"The kind of demands a friend can handle," Ellen said. "With all your talk about appeasement and keeping all the factions happy, everyone in town must know where you'd stand in a showdown. True?"

"I'm sure they do," Porter agreed.

"Then it can't have been easy for you. It's bound to get rougher. You'll be forced to fight."

Porter nodded. Was it Ellen's imagination, or had his eyes misted over with tears? He squared his shoulders abruptly and then turned the keys in the ignition. "Jerry has a right to expect that of me. We're old friends. In your case, he wanted to give fair warning."

He wouldn't have to warn me if he knew, Ellen thought. I'm not an old friend. I'm just someone who loves him.

Porter eased the car out of the hospital's parking lot into the quiet,

49

pine-edged streets of the town. He seemed eager to turn their conversation away from the depressing subject, saying, "Okay, prodigal daughter. You're back home. Where do we go? What would you like to see?"

It was impossible to tell Porter that she had already seen the only reason for her homecoming. But he seemed to understand when she told him that she was anxious to get home. The sooner she filled in the printed forms in her hand, the sooner he would be joined by an ally in the war between Barfield and a lone doctor.

4

ELLEN'S first taste of the poison that had infected Barfield came from Henry Barfield himself, and it came, ironically, in the form of a job offer.

From the day Ellen had met Porter Hubbard and they had formed their lonely alliance, he had become a frequent caller at the Whitaker home. Mom, who had bought a new house on a residential street just around the corner when she had expanded the old place, encouraged the visits. David, too, welcomed Porter's company. Every moment that Porter could spend away from his business and his numerous civic affairs was spent with Ellen.

He had taken her to a play at the junior college one evening, and it was in the auditorium lobby, afterwards, that Porter Hubbard whispered in her ear, "It had to happen sooner or later. There's no avoiding them now."

Seconds later, Ellen was being introduced to Henry and Carrie Barfield, people she had known only by sight before she left the town; people who had probably not known of her existence at the time.

Henry, a sparsely built man with thin brown strands of hair carefully distributed over a bald dome, had a face built along downsweeping lines that combined with extremely large ears to give him a peculiarly hound-doggish appearance. His wife towered over him, a rangy, hawkish woman with watery blue eyes. Her chemically bright hair, tortured into a coiffure that added unnecessary inches to her height, shrieked its yellow-pink loudness under the brilliant lights of the foyer.

For Porter's sake, Ellen hid her distaste for the pair and for all they represented. "I thought your daughter was wonderful," she said truthfully. "She's talented enough to be a professional actress."

The Barfield's smiled their appreciation with the practiced smiles that come easily to dedicated civic leaders. "How sweet of you to say that, dear," Carrie Barfield gushed.

"Wanted to be a fashion designer last time I talked to her," Porter said. "And an airline hostess the time before."

"Teen-agers!" Carrie held a bony, ring-bedecked hand to her forehead in mock horror. The laughter that followed was warm and affectionate; no one would have dreamed that the four people standing together making small talk were opponents in a battle that involved a man's future.

"You certainly chose a sensible course for yourself, Miss Whitaker," Henry Barfield said. "I always advise young people to choose a field where the demand exceeds the supply."

Ellen was startled to see the man's steely grey eyes focused on her. "I . . . didn't think you knew I'm a nurse."

Carrie shot a worshipful glance at her husband. "Henry's on the Hospital Board, my dear. The Board approves all new employees."

Porter nodded at Ellen, verifying the statement.

"Actually, you haven't started work yet," Henry said. "There's an excellent opening for an industrial nurse at the paper products plant. Extremely light duties and a salary considerably higher than what you can earn at the hospital." He shot a critical glance at Porter. "You see, the plant isn't operating in the red. Why don't you stop in and see me at my office, Miss Whitaker?" He started to draw a card from his billfold. "I'll send you over with . . ."

"Thank you, but I'm not interested," Ellen said.

There was a brief, uncomfortable silence, and then Porter said, "I'm a little surprised to see a Board member hijacking the hospital's personnel. Ellen's had surgical experience. You know how badly Dr. Sterling need helps in surgery."

The two faces that had been exuding good cheer a moment ago had become frozen slabs. "Hijacking is a rather strong word, Porter." Henry Barfield turned his attention back to Ellen. "Perhaps you should know, Miss Whitaker, that we anticipate . . . changes at the hospital. You might want to move to a position there later. Along with Dr. Grath."

Porter frowned. "Who's Dr. Grath?"

"An exceptionally well-qualified young physician," Henry said. "We expect him in town next week."

Porter's tone was agreeable, but his expression reflected caution. "Setting up a practice here? Good. With Dr. Vosbergh taking it easier — getting near retirement age — we can use another doctor. We could support several more."

"Dr. Grath isn't . . . prepared to open a private practice just yet," Henry said. A vindictive half-smile played around the corners of his mouth. "At present, he's accepted a position in industry. Medical services at the chemical plant."

"Henry sees to it that his employees have every possible benefit," Carrie said. "If any little thing happens, they'll have a doctor right there to . . . "

"What if something *big* happens?" Porter interrupted. "If they need hospital care, where will your doctor take his patients, Henry? To Templeton?"

"I should think that will be a matter for him to decide," Henry said. He threw a sickly smile at Ellen. "I don't think laymen should dictate to professional people."

Carrie Barfield reached out one of her chicken claw hands to squeeze Ellen's wrist. "Do think about the job Henry's offered you, my dear. A pretty girl like you . . . if you're anything like Lorna, I'm sure you love clothes and whatnot. Money isn't everything, but with that salary, good heavens . . . "

Ellen fixed her with a venomous

stare. "You're absolutely right, Mrs. Barfield. Money isn't everything. And the only interest I have in clothing right now is keeping my uniform clean."

Carrie attempted a little dismissive laugh, but it was obvious that Ellen's inference had not escaped her and that she was seething inside. "Well. Well, of course. It's wonderful to see so much idealism in young people. But perhaps if you knew . . . "

The foyer lights flicked off and on, and Ellen noticed that the crowd had thinned out.

"I think the janitor's inviting us to leave," Porter said. He nodded at the Barfields. "Good night, folks."

They responded politely, Henry adding his hope that Ellen would enjoy her return to Barfield. But no one could have warmed his hands on the atmosphere between them.

Porter waited until the couple had a long head start before he escorted Ellen out of the auditorium and towards the college's parking area. They were in his car before Porter said, "He's got Jerry's replacement all lined up, damn him. Bringing him to town and putting him on the payroll, waiting like a vulture for Jerry to topple over."

"Can he do that?" Ellen asked. "Force Dr. Sterling out?"

Porter started his car savagely, tyres shrieking against the asphalt paving as he tore out of the lot. "Jerry has a lifetime contract. Remember, Henry's father built the hospital because Jerry convinced him it was needed."

"Well, then . . . "

"No contract is ironbound. The hospital's supposed to be self-supporting. The way it's going, it'll break the city budget in a couple of years. Henry can claim mismanagement, incompetence, lack of public confidence." Porters fury was demonstrated in a screeching turn at the corner. "Jerry'd be supporting it with his inheritance if the money weren't all tied up in the courts. Pressure. Put enough pressure on a man and he'll make a mistake. That's what Henry's counting on."

"A medical mistake?"

"That would be all Henry needs. Never thought I'd see the day when he'd try to keep the calibre of the nursing service down. He was pretty impressed with your references."

"I wasn't impressed with his job."

Porter braked the car to a jarring halt at a street light. "Did you see his face when you made that remark about keeping your uniform clean? It did my heart good and I can't wait to tell Jerry about it. But, you know, you've crossed your Rubicon, honey. From now on, you're in the enemy camp, and no quarter."

"You weren't exactly the old pacifier yourself," Ellen reminded. "You called it for what it was. Hijacking. And asking him what hospital his company doctor's going to use . . ."

"There comes a time," Porter said. His arms slid easily over Ellen's shoulders. "There comes a time when peaceful negotiations start breaking down. Your army grows in strength and you start slugging. Ellen, you don't know how important you've become. To Jerry, to the hospital. To me."

The rapport of their common cause had not left Ellen untouched. But she sat rigidly under the casual embrace, reminding herself that Porter was too precious as a friend to be encouraged beyond that point. The light had turned green and she was grateful for an impatient honk from the car behind them.

Providentially, too, Ellen's brother was pulling up in front of the house at the time they arrived. It was too late to ask Porter in, and parking outside was precluded as David strolled up to the Lincoln to ask their opinion of the play. After their brief chat, it wasn't even necessary for Porter to see Ellen to the door.

Otherwise, Ellen was certain, she would have been faced with the problem of telling Porter Hubbard

that she didn't want him to kiss her
good night.

* * *

Ellen's encounter with Henry Barfield
was direct. There were other incidents,
other conversations aimed at the same
result, but the sources were more
hypocritical and more insidious. Henry
was a powerful lion, roaring his
animosity; the others were termites,
gnawing away at the foundations of
Jerry Sterling's dream for Barfield
Hospital.

There were the four clubwomen
having lunch at Mom Whitaker's
Dinner House one afternoon. Ellen sat
at a nearby corner table, helping Mom
out during this waiting period by proof-
reading a new menu. She hadn't wanted
to eavesdrop, but the high-pitched
female voices could have been heard
by anyone in the large dining room:

" . . . so wonderful to see Mrs.
Agnew home."

61

"Yes, isn't it? She came out of that operation like a new woman."

"Well, she was wise. It's a shame, though, that we have to go all the way to Templeton to get proper care. Still, I'd rather do that than risk my life."

"I told my daughter that. Exactly that. I just hope when her baby's due her husband's home to drive her all that way."

"Terrible, to have to risk a long drive like that. Couldn't she go to Dr. Vosbergh?"

"And take the chance he'd be off fishing somewhere? Let that monster deliver the baby?"

"I don't know how that Sterling person got away with it. First marrying that poor girl, getting himself a hospital and then all that money. My husband says we ought to get up a committee. Run him out of town, since the law's so blind."

"I'd leave it to Mr. Barfield. He knows how to get things done."

"Through the City Council. Yes, we

don't want any vigilante groups making a scandal."

"I still say he bribed somebody, going off scot-free the way he did."

"Wouldn't surprise me. Maybe that's how he got to call himself a doctor, too. Probably paid some quack school for a phony diploma. I tell you, if I had to travel to Timbuktu, I wouldn't set foot in that hospital. Not if I was *dying*."

"I didn't know he wasn't really a doctor. *Really?*"

"Well, I'm not completely sure, but I've heard a lot of people say . . . "

An uncontrollable rage swept over Ellen. "*It's not true!*" She was on her feet, her voice shrilling above the quiet voices of the other patrons in the room. "How can you sit here and repeat such vicious lies? Dr. Sterling headed his class at one of the best med schools in the country! He was Chief Resident in Surgery at one of the highest-rated hospitals in the East! And he doesn't own the hospital — he doesn't *have* any money! He's the most dedicated . . . "

Shaking with anger, she found herself suddenly wordless. There was too much to say, and yet in the face of those blatant lies, nothing at all that would make any impression. The quartet was eyeing her with indignant, icy disapproval, and she was aware that the other people in the room were staring, too. The silence that followed was like a massive, oppressive weight closing down upon her from the ceiling.

Ellen turned away, hot tears blistering her face. On her way to the sanctity of her mother's office, she heard the silent void filled by the buzzing of animated voices. Mom had been supervising a private luncheon on the second floor; evidently she had heard Ellen's tirade and hurried downstairs, because one of the four women was saying, "Frankly, Mrs. Whitaker, if we can't enjoy our lunch here without being listened to and screamed at, there are other places in town, you know. I think the women's Club will agree with me."

Her face burning, Ellen listened to

her mother's apologies. They were important customers; she appreciated the club's patronage; her daughter was a bit high-strung and in need of a vacation . . . she was sorry, sorry, sorry.

Later, when Mom had joined her in the partitioned office area, Ellen repeated the words. "I'm sorry. I shouldn't have lost my temper. But if you'd heard the vile things they were saying . . . "

"When they come here and pay for their meals, they have a right to say whatever they please," Mom said firmly. "Mrs. Long was absolutely right. You invaded their privacy and you were unbelievably rude."

Ellen buried her face in her hands, unable to reply.

She felt her mother's hand closing over her shoulder. "Your father would have done exactly the same thing. Bellowed at them. I've seen Porter talk to people who cast slurs at Dr. Sterling. Polite, soft-spoken, reasonable. Allowing them their say, like a gentleman, and then telling them why he disagreed. People *listen* to Porter. They don't leave the room in a huff."

There was nothing for Ellen to do but to repeat her apologies and assure Mom that it would never happen again. Porter Hubbard knew this town; even people who disagreed with him liked Porter. Ellen had ignored his advice and compounded a bad situation. With friends like her, Jerry Sterling didn't need enemies.

Ellen remembered the lesson at the post office the next morning when a young factory worker took his copy of the *Barfield Register* out of his post-office box. A front page story in the bi-weekly paper owned by Henry Barfield was captioned: NEW RESIDENT SUCCUMBS AT LOCAL HOSPITAL.

The workman turned to his companion, another young man wearing overalls embroidered with the paper-products company's insignia. "How many more thay gonna kill in that joint before they get ridda that quack doctor?"

There was only a doleful shaking of the other man's head.

Tell them the truth, Ellen's insides screamed. Porter had told her about the death two days before. Henry's kept press referred to the dead man as a newcomer, subtly indicating youth. The article failed to reveal that he was ninety-two years old, that he had suffered four previous heart attacks, and was pronounced dead on arrival at Barfield Hospital. Neither Jerry Sterling nor Dr. Vosbergh, who had been phoned by the man's relatives and had sent an ambulance for the stricken old man — neither of the doctors had ever seen him before his body was carried into the Emergency Room. Yet the story mentioned only Jerry's name: 'Mr. Allister was being attended by Dr. Sterling at the time of his sudden demise.'

It was a monstrous dream, Ellen

kept telling herself: a nightmare in broad daylight. And later that day she was talking to the middle-aged lady who came to the Whitaker house to pick up the ironing when she noticed her arthritis-racked fingers. Ellen said, "You must have a terrible time working with those swollen joints, Mrs. Strout. Are you getting medical care?"

Even that pathetic soul joined the chorus of misunderstanding and hostility! "Don't talk these local doctors to me, young lady. I used to get some relief from Dr. Vosbergh, but I ain't goin' back to no doctor that'd have truck with a killer."

"Mrs. Strout, you know that . . . "

"Bled the money from that old man, then when he got what he wanted, jest threw that poor child's body in a ditch. Couldn't even do *that* kind of operation right."

Ellen struggled to keep calm — to do it Porter's way. "Well, now, some people have a way of spreading ugly rumours, Mrs. Strout. But fair-minded people, like you . . . "

"I'm not sayin' he did it for sure. That's all past history. What I care about is, what's he doin' *now*!"

Ellen opened her mouth to reply, but the woman supplied her own answer:

"Look at the paper today, if you want to know. Listen, honey, help me get this bundle into my jalopy, will you? I got all I can do to walk, the way my bones are killin' me."

All over town, the lies proliferating like cancerous cells, destroying Jerry Sterling in their malignant growth. What could he do?

There was no way for him to fight the rumour-mongers. The only accuser who was not faceless was Henry Barfield, and Jerry was powerless against him. That leaves Porter Hubbard, Ellen thought. And me.

It was a battle that drew her constantly closer to Porter. Urged by her mother, encouraged by David, she found herself looking forward to the hours spent with Jerry Sterling's best friend, yet cringing with guilt because this was Porter's greatest value to her: he was close to Jerry. Together, they talked about Jerry, planned their strategy to help Jerry, shared their admiration for Jerry's courage.

And the evening before Ellen was to start working at Barfield Hospital, when Porter's arms fell naturally and easily around her, she could not summon the strength to resist his gentle kiss. It was a restrained, almost brotherly kiss. But Porter's eyes implored her to invite another, and Porter's affectionate smile and sudden release of her body told Ellen that he would be patient. Wordlessly, his expression told her that a man who has waited a long time for love learns to be patient.

Working helped. Being busy, and seeing the positive aspects of Jerry Sterling's position, partially erased the vicious gossips from Ellen's memory.

Under the young doctor's direction, Barfield Hospital was an island of purposeful calm surrounded by a turbulent sea of hysteria. If the number of patients admitted was small, the staff was small, too, and with Jerry's insistence that every patient get the most conscientious care possible, there was no time for idle speculation about the opposing forces.

* * *

There were three incidents during Ellen's second month on the job which proved to her that the conflict surrounding Jerry Sterling was more complex than she had imagined. If nothing else, she learned that the participants could not be divided, like the characters in a western movie, into simple categories like the 'good guys' and the 'bad guys'.

First, there was the matter of Dr. Vosbergh. A white-haired, florid-faced elephant of a man, he was by temperament, if not circumstance, the old-fashioned horse-and-buggy doctor who traded his services for produce.

Observing him closely, Ellen considered him an honest and conscientious doctor, if not a gifted one. Jerry Sterling's criticism might have been more severe; Dr. Vosbergh assumed that his vast and varied smalltown experience was more valuable than any of the new developments constantly emerging in the medical field. His education had ended when he nailed up his shingle. Nevertheless, in doctor-deprived Barfield, he was a needed asset.

Ellen exchanged brief pleasantries with Dr. Vosbergh one afternoon, meeting him outside the administration office. Seconds afterwards carrying a medications report Dr. Sterling had asked to see, Ellen found the latter at his desk, a stunned expression on his face.

Usually, Ellen tried to avoid personal references, but Jerry's pallor alarmed her and she asked, "Is something wrong, Doctor? You don't look well."

"I don't feel well," he admitted, "but there's nothing you can do about it, thanks. He's quitting."

"Dr. Vosbergh? But — why?"

"A man has a right to retire," Jerry said. His explanation didn't sound convincing. "He's not sixty-five yet. Sixty-one, I believe. But, as he says, it's been a long, hard grind and his heart's been giving him trouble."

"Nothing serious?"

"I don't know. I offered to examine him, but you know doctors. They draw the line at being patients. I'll probably be as stubborn about my own health at his age."

Jerry had never sounded more affable, nor taken time for this sort of idle banter. He was clearly covering up a shocking disappointment.

"He's giving up his practice, then?" Ellen scowled. "I don't like to criticise a doctor, but wouldn't you think he'd have turned his practice over to someone else? Sold it, or brought in another doctor? This leaves the town without a single private physician."

"He's not giving up his practice

completely," Jerry said. He feigned interest in a record book on his desk, indicating that the conversation was getting uncomfortable and he wanted to end it. "Dr. Vosbergh has his practice at his home. He'll still see his old patients, but he won't be accepting any new ones. And . . . he'll be relieved of the strain of going back and forth from the hospital. It leaves me without an assistant in surgery, of course."

Ellen asked the same question Porter had posed to Henry Barfield about the new company doctor. "What if one of his patients need hospitalisation?"

"I didn't have the guts to ask him that," Jerry said after a long pause. "I like Dr. Vosbergh. Whatever his plans are, whatever reason for them, I wasn't going to embarrass him."

"You'll need another doctor here. A staff doctor to relieve you, if nothing else. You need an anaesthetist. The hospital can't function without attending doctors who bring their private patients to . . ."

"We need a lot of things," Jerry said quietly. "Most of the Board members don't seem to agree." He looked up at Ellen, and for the first time she saw a look of desperation in the dark eyes. "Dr. Vosbergh aside, what would lure a young doctor to set up a new practice in a town that's terrified of its own hospital? Ellen, what would happen if an epidemic ever hit Barfield, God forbid?"

She left him shortly afterwards, unable to provide answers to his agonising questions. Was Dr. Vosbergh's semi-retirement analogous to rats deserting a sinking ship? Had Henry Barfield exerted some unknown pressure on a doctor who readily admitted he was tired and preferred fishing to looking after patients? And if failure was inevitable, in asking that question about an epidemic, wasn't Jerry Sterling weighing his own responsibility to the community? It was because of him that the people of Barfield shunned the hospital that belonged to them.

Was he wondering if his struggle was doomed . . . wondering if staying here was even justified?

There was the possibility that he might quit. He had been dealt another body blow, and Ellen empathised with his depression. But, shamefully, she gave less thought that evening to these negative facts than to a single hope-stirring word. For the first time since she had come back to work beside him, Jerry Sterling had called her *Ellen*.

Dr. Vosbergh had been counted with the 'good guys'. Ellen was uncertain about his status now. She had also included the entire Barfield family in that oversimplified pigeonholing. She learned, the next morning, that she had been wrong.

David's favourite girl, Joan Eliot, had been admitted to the hospital the night before, suffering a possible concussion. David had been with her at the college's indoor swimming pool when the accident had happened; doing a demonstration of shallow-water diving, she had misjudged the depth on the shallow end of the pool and struck her head on the tiled bottom. David had pulled her out of the water, bleeding and unconscious. He had not hesitated a moment in rushing her to Barfield Hospital.

Fortunately, the laceration on Joan's forehead was minor, but her parents had agreed with Dr. Sterling that Joan should remain hospitalised until even the slightest possibility of a concussion was ruled out. Mr. Eliot, a biology teacher at the junior college, and his wife were strong partisans in the Sterling camp.

Ellen's morning arrival found Joan not only in good condition but in high spirits, and the only problem at the hospital seemed to be keeping David Whitaker from camping at her bedside.

He was in the room that afternoon with another of Joan's friends when Ellen came to remind them that visiting hours were over.

"Dave, tell your sister she's a

spoilsport," Joan laughed, thumbing her nose at Ellen.

"I've got to change the queen's halo." Ellen set a tray of fresh bandages and antiseptic solution on the table next to Joan's bed. "Everybody scoot. Doctor's orders."

'Everybody' consisted only of David and a placid, beautifully groomed girl who smiled at Ellen and said, "I'm not getting into any argument with Doc Jerry. When he thinks something's *right* he doesn't put up with any nonsense."

The girl had long, straight, shining brown hair and eyes of a disturbingly familiar grey shade. It took Ellen a moment to recall where she had seen her before; on the stage at the college auditorium. "You're Lorna Barfield, aren't you?"

"Oh, I'm sorry," David apologised. "I thought you knew each other." He turned to Lorna. "She knows *you*, but I guess you've never met my sister Ellen"

"We probably saw each other around

town," Lorna said. "Anyway, I've heard about you." Before Ellen could assume that she had got her preview from the elder Barfield, Lorna added, "From Joanie. And Porter Hubbard. He thinks you're the living end." Lorna smiled. "He's my vocational adviser."

Joan made a wry face. "By that she means every time she changes her mind about what she's going to be, she tells Porter about it and he laughs."

There was an animated and flattering discussion of Porter Hubbard, with all three of the college students agreeing that he was 'a swinger' who was not only respected by the business community but by 'the kids'.

"Everybody's crazy about Porter and he's crazy about Ellen," Joan said. "Nice going. You could do a lot worse, Nurse."

"I have a faint suspicion I'm being shoved," Ellen said. She changed the subject abruptly, reminding David and Lorna again that visiting hours were over.

Lorna checked her watch. "Is it really that late? I've got to get to my rehearsal."

"Another play?" Ellen asked.

"It's a one-acter," Lorna told her. "All the junior colleges in the state have this one-act play competition in June. It's a big deal — we're all going to Denver in a chartered bus — the whole cast, and any other kids who want to go. I've just got a small part in this one, but it's going to be fabulous, with talent scouts and all kinds of important people there."

"Did you get your dad's okay?" Joan asked.

Lorna sighed. "Yes, finally. Sort of." She addressed an explanation to Ellen. "My folks associate acting with sin. You see, my cousin Naomi had some idea about being an actress for a while there. Before she married Doc. I guess you know . . . none of her ideas turned out to be too cool." Remarkably poised for a girl not yet out of her teens, Lorna seemed neither embarrassed nor evasive about the subject of her glamorous cousin's tragic death. "So I'm stuck with trying to convince my folks that being in a play doesn't necessarily make you a tramp."

Ellen drew a sharp breath at the frank evaluation. Lorna was looking at her as though she expected some sort of response, and Ellen dredged her mind for a non-committal statement. "I didn't know Naomi too well. All I remember is that she was beautiful and she . . . liked to have fun."

"So do I," Lorna said quietly. she spoke as though she might be talking to herself, her voice simultaneously bitter and sorrowful. "Only I don't want the guy I marry to pay for it for the rest of his life. I tried to get that across to her. I'm still trying to get it across to . . . some people I know."

Lorna and David left after that, taking time only to assure Joan that they would return that evening.

Ellen removed the dressing from

Joan's forehead, her hands strangely unsteadied by the encounter. Lorna had referred to 'Doc Jerry' with unmistakable respect, even a wistful fondness.

Joan Eliot seemed to sense the question in Ellen's mind. "Did you notice the way Lorna looked up and down the corridor before she left the room? She came here to see me against family orders, I know that. Her folks would have a fit if they found out she talked to Dr. Sterling."

Ellen held fast to an ingrained code, avoiding personal discussions of doctors, patients, and visitors. "This may hurt just a little, Joan."

Joan ignoring the stinging antiseptic. "It must be rough. I mean, I love my mom and dad, but we don't always get along. Think of the hell Lorna must go through, loving her folks and *hating* all the crumby things they do."

★ ★ ★

A third incident that realigned the forces opposing and supporting Jerry Sterling took place near the end of May.

Although there was no M.D., anaesthesiologist on the staff, Porter had persuaded the Hospital Board to hire a nurse trained in anaesthesia. Still, without a doctor to assist him, and with no attending doctors bringing private patients to the hospital, the operating rooms were unused. Barfield Hospital was functioning more as a sanatorium than a complete medical facility, and Ellen sensed that Jerry was almost ready to admit defeat.

There were exactly twelve patients in the hospital on the morning that Porter Hubbard, looking even more jaunty than usual, met Ellen in one of the corridors. With him was a rather colourless, extremely serious-visaged young man whose small face was dominated by disproportionately large shell-rimmed glasses.

On her way to a linen supply closet,

Ellen merely smiled and wished Porter good morning; his fast pace in the direction of Jerry's office indicated that he wasn't going to stop for introductions.

After she had changed the bedding for two of the patients in her small ward, Ellen stepped out into the corridor and saw Porter leaving the hospital alone. More than an hour later, the stranger was still in the administration office, and shortly after noon Ellen saw the two men making a thorough inspection of the hospital.

Just before she was due to go off duty, Ellen was completing a medications report, when the doctor came up to the nurses' station. He had just escorted the mysterious guest to the exit doors, and there was an air of hopeful enthusiasm about him. It was almost the first time Ellen had seen Jerry Sterling smile. "I hope you haven't forgotten O.R. procedures, Miss Whitaker. It looks as though we'll be doing surgery again soon."

Ellen returned the smile. "I suppose you know everyone's dying of curiosity, Doctor."

"That was Dr. Grath. He's starting a new general practice in town, and he'll be available to assist in surgery. Starting whenever he's needed."

"Dr. Grath?" Ellen had conjured up visions of Henry Barfield's company doctor: a villainous character waiting like a buzzard for a chance to take over the hospital. "I thought he was working at one of the plants."

"He was, until . . . I think he realised that it was a sham position. I've no doubt he was talked into the job on the basis of some rosy promises for the future. Fortunately he's not a man who accepts everything he hears. He's a doctor, not a puppet."

"I understood he wasn't able to afford setting himself up in practice yet."

"He wasn't," Jerry said. "He had quite a struggle financing his education. Fact is, he's still in debt. But with the need for a G.P. here in Barfield, loaning him the money for offices and equipment wasn't much of a risk. Luckily, when he decided the job at the plant could easily be handled by a nurse, he started checking around. And he approached the right man."

"Porter Hubbard." It wasn't a question; Ellen had anticipated the name."

"Right." Jerry's enthusiasm was dampened for a moment. "I told Dr. Grath the same things I tried to tell you, Miss Whitaker. He's sticking his neck out. In his case, the pressure will be worse; you can imagine how gracefully Henry Barfield accepted his resignation."

Ellen rolled her eyes ceilingwards. "I'm glad I wasn't there."

"I prepared the doctor for resistance to the hospital, too. He's going to lose patients because of it." Jerry shook his head in disbelief. "He said he knew that. I had forgotten that there are still some amazingly courageous doctors around."

"I could have told you that," Ellen said quietly. "I work for one."

Jerry's eyes met hers for an instant, then swerved away in embarrassment. "I don't have a choice. Dr. Grath did. Now, if we hold firm and keep improving the quality of our services . . ." He looked out beyond the glass doors at the end of the corridor, towards the church, the business district, the town. "They'll stop risking their lives, wasting precious minutes to overcrowd the hospital in Templeton." Then, breaking out of the sombre mood, Jerry smiled again. "This may be the turning point. All because a doctor couldn't go on feeling useless and contacted the president of the Hospital Board."

It was the other way around, Ellen was certain. Porter Hubbard had spared Jerry's pride, insisted that Dr. Grath go along with his version of the meeting, telling Jerry that the first move hadn't been made by Porter. But Ellen remembered Porter's expression in the lobby of the college auditorium; politely listening to Henry Barfield crow about the replacement he had lined up for the hospital. And, with equal politeness, seeking out Dr. Grath and telling him that he was being used in a plot to destroy another dedicated physician.

In the Whitaker living room that evening, Ellen forced the admission from Porter.

"It would have happened sooner or later," he said lightly. "Let's say I just . . . speeded the process up a little. Jerry's had enough hitting him without having to feel constantly obligated for favours."

"But setting Dr. Grath up in practice . . . "

"A perfectly sound investment," Porter said. "Jerry sees it that way, too, so stop trying to make me feel heroic." The cornflower-blue eyes lighted up, reflecting a sudden grin. "Besides, it was worth more than I invested to see Henry at the Men's Club luncheon this afternoon. He didn't mention Dr. Grath, but I noticed he didn't have dessert. Any time a man passes up that terrific Whitaker strawberry pie, he's got to be fuming inside."

It was a mistake to laugh, sharing Porter's triumph, or to look at him with deeply felt affection and tell him he was wonderful. Porter responded by taking Ellen's hand into his own, admitting that since his best friend's bitter experience he had been wary about women, but that he had been terribly lonely. Lonely, and waiting for someone to come along. Someone he could trust and respect . . . and love.

"I'm a long way from being 'wonderful'," Porter said huskily. "But you'd give me something to live up to, Ellen. If you were my wife, I'd knock myself out trying."

He paused, not reaching out to take Ellen in his arms, waiting hopefully for her acceptance.

Like someone drowning, Ellen recalled her own loneliness and her own desperate need for love. To Jerry, she was still no more than a dutiful nurse — at best, a loyal friend. The wounds he had suffered in the name of love might never heal. Was she to spend the rest of her life waiting for him to see her as a woman, the way she had waited during those first painful pangs of adolescent love? What was it Joan had said? 'Everybody's crazy about Porter and *he's* crazy about Ellen. Nice going. You could do a lot worse, Nurse.' It was true. It was all true, and yet . . .

She hesitated too long. "It's all right," Porter said. He lifted his massive frame from the sofa and started towards the door. "I shouldn't have mentioned it."

Ellen remained motionless. "I'm sorry, Porter. It would be easier if I weren't so fond of you. As it is I . . ."

He stood near the door for a few seconds longer, his back turned to Ellen. "I understand. Maybe if I weren't such an insensitive clod, I'd have understood sooner." Porter turned around slowly, barely enunciating the name. "Jerry?"

Ellen closed her eyes, lowering her head.

She couldn't reply, and there was no need to. Porter crossed the room, extended one of his big hands, and ruffled her hair in a gesture that might have come from David. "Don't look so miserable. It's not the end of the world. It's one of those things . . . you know?"

She was crying, and Porter didn't lift her spirits by his bravado. Cheerfully, as though he had just received an encouraging piece of news, he said, "I'm all for him, too — remember? It'll be an easy fight now. A fella's got a woman who *loves* him on his side — how can we miss?"

5

PORTER'S optimistic prediction came face to face with grim reality two days later.

Dr. Sterling and Ellen were summoned to the Emergency Room early in the morning, to be met by a couple who might have stepped from a past century.

The man, bearded and gaunt, was dressed in a faded blue work shirt and worn denim overalls that sagged over a pair of badly stooped shoulders. His face might have been carved out of granite.

His wife, too, had a gnarled, misshapen appearance, like a scrub bush that has been battered and beaten out of shape by the elements. She wore an ankle-length dress of some drab, coarse material, and her wispy hair was partially covered by a black sunbonnet.

By their dress, Ellen recognised them immediately as members of a small fanatical sect that had isolated itself in a rugged mountain community some twenty-six miles from Barfield. A glance at the admittance form that a nurse had filled in revealed that they were named Eldridge.

Jerry Sterling's surveyal of the strange pair was cursory. His attention, and Ellen's, went immediately to the still form that lay stretched on one of the examining tables. The boy, perhaps ten or eleven years old, was dressed in the same dark, old-fashioned garb as the people who had brought him in. Thin and undernourished, his frail body moved only slightly as Ellen placed a cool hand on his forehead; his flesh felt raging hot to her touch, and a whimpering moan came through his cracked lips.

"Devil's got inside him," the man said. He had a voice that recalled rough sandpaper. "We been starvin' Satan out an' holdin' meetin's over Noah two days now, but it ain't worked. We're payin' the wages fer our sins."

"Deacon says it's a worse sin to take him outten the temple," the woman whispered. "All that moanin', three days an' nights . . . I just couldn't stand no more. We brung him in on the wagon . . . "

While the parents related their shocking story, Jerry started his examination, palpating the boy's abdomen. Ellen checked, then reported a failing pulse and a soaring temperature.

When he announced his diagnosis, Jerry's face looked drained of its colour. He wanted Dr. Grath's confirmation, he said, but the Eldridge's son was suffering from acute appendicitis. "Why didn't you bring him here when the pains began?" Jerry demanded. "We would have removed the diseased organ immediately, before we had peritonitis to deal with."

"We don't hold with cuttin' into the flesh," Mr. Eldridge said. "We don't even hold with medicine." Fright overcame his fanatical prejudice, and he must have realised the awkwardness of his presence in a hospital. "We figgered — jest this one time, if there was some pills, say, you could give our boy . . . "

"There isn't anything except an operation that can save your son," Jerry said. His anger with the parents' neglect softened; anger would not penetrate that wall of conditioned dread of their abysmal ignorance. "The devil can take the form of a *poison*," he said. Patience straining his nerves, he explained a ruptured organ and the resulting toxemia in phrases calculated to fit with the Eldridges' views of a vengeful God and bodily possession by demons.

They listened, stupidly, their eyes glazed by fear, intermittently darting frantic glances in the direction of the child they had starved and prayed over, then loaded into a horse-drawn cart for a rough, twenty-odd-mile ride to the sinful city. Believing as they did, terrified of hellfire and damnation, their decision to break the decrees of their warped religion must have been made at an unimaginable cost. They had been motivated by love, Jerry knew; he appealed to that love with carefully calculated words, never unaware, Ellen was certain, of the inexorable ticking of the clock on the wall.

Guilt was still tearing at the Eldridges twenty minutes later, when they signed their permission for an appendectomy. During the gruelling delay, Ellen had managed to reach Dr. Grath by telephone. With another nurse, she prepared to move Noah Eldridge to a bed near the O.R.

Ellen was at the bedside, setting up an I.V. stand, while the two doctors consulted.

"Massive therapy with antibiotics and sulfonamides," Jerry said. "Restoring the fluid balance, of course." He muttered the next words savagely. "I wonder how many times they've had to starve the kid to drive out 'devils' in the past ten years. He's so weak that . . . "

"Whole blood?" Dr. Grath asked.

"We started to get a type and cross match," Jerry told him. "The parents drew the line at blood transfusion. Religious grounds."

The new doctor made a shuttering gesture. "I don't have to give you my opinion of the patient as an operative risk, Doctor."

Jerry was covering the boy, studying the pinched face and the scrawny, undernourished body outlined by the sheet. "Don't you wish you could give me an alternative?" He stood at the bedside a moment longer, not weighing a decision (for without the appendectomy the child was doomed), but probably projecting himself forward, foreseeing the consequences of failure. "I'm going to schedule him for eight tomorrow morning. That is — if you'll scrub in to assist, Dr. Grath."

Jerry knew what he was asking; it would be the younger doctor's first operation in a town where the operating surgeon and the hospital were suspect. The prognosis was hardly favourable; to take the time to build up the boy's strength might only mean allowing the poisons at work in his body to take their toll.

Yet Jerry seemed to know, too, what Dr. Grath's answer would be. He had said that the newcomer was not a puppet. Neither was he a statistician who calculated personal risk, or a politician who avoided it. Without his help, a child would die.

"Of course I'll scrub," Dr. Grath said.

Jerry Sterling had expected the reply; the man was a *doctor*.

6

AN experienced anaesthesiologist, an M.D. with years of practice, would have been apprehensive. The nurse anaesthetist, Miss Llewelyn, seemed almost paralysed by fear. "He's so frail," she whispered to Ellen while Noah Eldridge was being prepped for the operation. "Just a breath too much ether, and . . . "

Miss Llewelyn was steadied by the swift, skilful knowingness of the operating team. It seemed to Ellen, too, that Jerry Sterling and Dr. Grath had been co-ordinating their every move in hundreds of operations before this one, and that she had been beside them, responding to their crisp requests for instruments, anticipating their needs as her eyes recorded the movement of their gloved hands in the operational field. They worked together like extensions of a single mind.

Several times, seeing the extent of the damage caused by delay, the doctors' eyes met in darting glances, registering their disgust with ignorance. Most of the time, the expressions above their masks were only intensely thoughtful and alert.

"*Hemostat.*"

"*Hemostat, please.*"

"*Gauze sponges . . .* "

"*Clamps.*"

"*Sutures.*"

"*Right-angled clamp.*"

"*Pulse.*"

"*It's thready, Doctor. His pressure's down . . .* "

"*He's hanging on. It's ligated now . . . fine.*"

"*If we could only start a unit . . .* "

They were nearing the end, their speed accelerated by the urgency of their small patient's ebbing strength. Jerry Sterling was completing closure of the subcutaneous tissue when Miss

Llewelyn cried out, "I don't get a pulse, Doctor! I'm not getting *anything*."

"He's arrested." Dr. Grath made a quick check of the gauges. "There's no blood pressure."

"I don't feel a pulse in the aorta, either." Jerry sterling's voice echoed through the tile-covered room, hollow, awed by the sudden terrifying possibility. But his next words were firm. "Finish the closure, Doctor. I'm going to massage the heart. Miss Whitaker, adrenalin." The next order was barked at Miss Llewelyn. "Start a unit of blood, stat!"

Miss Llewelyn eyes looked at him with horror. "Doctor, we aren't set up for . . . "

Jerry's gasp was audible to everyone around the table. His command had been automatic; now he remembered. They weren't set up; they *couldn't* set up now. Transfusion was a slim lifeline, but it was their single hope for pouring new life into Noah Eldridge's limp body. Not to give him that chance was

murder. *And they couldn't.* Expressly
forbidden to do so by the patient's
family, they *couldn't!*

A grim silence enveloped the table,
but the effort to save the boy's life
was uninterrupted. Dr. Sterling tried.
Frantically, desperately, using every
means known to him, while Ellen held
her breath and Miss Llewelyn's eyes
flooded with tears at her helplessness,
he tried.

He was still working feverishly ten
minutes later when Dr. Grath reaffirmed
what everyone in the O.R. already
knew. They had witnessed the nightmare that haunts every surgeon; a
patient had been lost on the operating
table.

"He's gone," Dr. Grath said quietly.

Another long, unendurable period
of time elapsed before Jerry Sterling
turned away from the lifeless little
form, pulling off his gloves, then lifting
his hands to his face.

Miss Llewelyn was weeping silently,
her back to the table. Dr. Grath stood

immobile, shaking his head from side to side, uncomprehendingly. Ellen's eyes followed Jerry on his way out of the O.R., every atom in her body yearning to console him, to give him strength for the ordeal that lay ahead.

She couldn't follow him into the corridor, of course. There were heart-breaking duties to attend to here in this white-walled room that had suddenly become a chill sepulchre. As agonisingly as she wanted to be with him, Jerry would be alone when he faced the boy's parents. Alone, and unable to communicate to a grief-crazed mother that he had wanted nothing more than to give her back a recovered, living child.

His pain transferred itself to Ellen. The others knew it, too; any doctor or nurse would have felt it. Anyone in the world who heard the shrieking, anguished cries from the corridor:

"*You killed him! You're a tool of the devil! You murdered our boy . . . our little boy . . . oh, Lord, our little boy!*"

7

JERRY STERLING'S self-castigation was excruciating enough without the added venom piled upon him by his enemies in Barfield.

"I should have waited," Ellen heard him cry the next morning. His face showed the ravages of a sleepless night. He had not stopped pacing the floor since Ellen's entry into his office. "He was too weak. I should have . . . "

"Dr. Grath says you *couldn't* have waited," Ellen said firmly. "The boy should have been started on blood the day before, but you couldn't do that."

If Jerry was listening to Ellen's arguments, he showed no response. His mind was reviewing every detail of the case, Ellen guessed. Over and over, asking himself what had gone wrong, what he had neglected, where he had failed.

Ellen left him at three o'clock, tortured and unresponsive, still asking himself the silent, unanswerable questions.

★ ★ ★

Porter Hubbard's visit to the Whitaker home that night was not unexpected. He had rallied to Jerry's side soon after word of the tragedy reached him, staying with him most of the night before. Today he had phoned Ellen twice at the hospital, asking how Jerry was holding up under the strain. During the second call, he had said, "I'll stop by tonight, if you're going to be at home. It may be late."

It *was* late. Mom had gone to bed, and David was yawning in an attempt to keep Ellen company while she waited.

David greeted Porter at the door. "Hi, c'mon in. We were about to give you up."

"Hello, Dave . . . Ellen." Porter followed David into the living room, throwing a folded newspaper on the coffee table. "Sorry about keeping you up. I wanted to pick *that* up before I came by."

"I'm afraid to look at it," Ellen said.

David had pulled up a chair and reached for the paper. "Tomorrow's *Barfield Register*, uh? What'd you do, Porter, stop at the press room?"

Porter sank into the sofa near Ellen. "I wanted to get a preview of what everyone in town's going to be reading in the morning. If that rag was a daily, they'd have been reading it *this* morning." He pounded one fist into an open palm. "What does Henry want, a lynch mob?"

"That bad?" Ellen asked.

David continued to stare at the front page. "Man. This is really hitting below the belt." He looked towards Ellen, handing her the newspaper. "Oh — here. Porter didn't bring this for me to read."

Moments later, Ellen half-wished Porter hadn't brought the newspaper at all. Henry Barfield's paper didn't accuse Jerry Sterling of malpractice; the publisher was too shrewd about legal matters to risk implying that the surgeon was responsible for young Noah Eldridge's death. The message was distorted not by what was said, but by what was left unsaid.

"What can we do?" Ellen asked. The old Whitaker trait threatened her with explosion. "There's got to be something we can do."

Porter had evidently been thinking about positive steps. "I'm going to demand a full report in the next issue. Henry's going to discover there are merchants in this town who'll back me up. A very few always *did* believe in Jerry; a few I've been able to reach, day by day, through the past year. And I know some who want Jerry out, but won't advertise in a paper that distorts the truth. This town's going to read it straight next Friday."

Porter's slow, plodding, patient way was bearing some fruit, at least. It was a better method than the impetuous scheme David proposed: "We ought to call a meeting for patients Dr. Sterling's helped. They'd rally to . . ."

"You can't make a carnival out of a doctor's career," Ellen argued. "You'd have dissenters, arguments — a kangaroo trial that would drag his name through the mud and wouldn't solve anything. Either that, or the people he's done the most for wouldn't turn out."

"People in a small town are afraid to buck popular opinion. Especially in a case like this, with emotions running high," Porter said. "We have to continue a conservative approach. The thing will die down faster if we don't try to pit neighbours against each other in a free-for-all." He got up from the sofa, crossing the room with the same agitated strides Ellen had seen Jerry Sterling taking earlier. "At heart, they mean well. They'll do the right thing, once they understand."

Ellen glanced at her brother. David was nodding, concurring; he had been the first to tell her that the people of Barfield were 'good'.

Porter had reseated himself on the arm of an over-stuffed chair. He had calmed himself, saving his energies for the planning of a strategy. Filling his pipe, he said, "I've called a special meeting of the Hospital Board for tomorrow morning at ten. Jerry usually attends, but I know he has an operation scheduled at that time."

"He did have a partial cholecystectomy. Dr. Vosbergh's patient. Her family had her transferred to Templeton Hospital this afternoon." Sick at heart, Ellen remembered accompanying the woman to the ambulance. "I couldn't reach Dr. Vosbergh to sign Mrs. Schmidt out, but her husband said it didn't matter. He'd consulted another doctor in Templeton."

"I'll ask Jerry to stay away, then," Porter said. "I'm going to let the other Board members know exactly what happened in this Eldridge case."

"You told me once all of them

were hand-picked by Henry," Ellen reminded him.

"I've got to make them see that destroying Jerry with the hope of replacing him is liable to ruin the hospital for good." Porter lighted his pipe and puffed on it, scowling. "Trouble is, Henry knows why I called the meeting. He'll come armed with figures from the City Council, figures on the low rate of admission. I can't refute the financial facts. For all I know, he's liable to produce a petition demanding Jerry's dismissal."

A gloomy pall had settled over the room. "I guess now we know how Dr. Sterling's folks felt when they moved to Utah," David said. "They loved it here. It was just . . . things got so bad for them, they couldn't take it any more. It looked too hopeless." David thumbed at the newspaper in Ellen's lap. "Like it does now."

Ellen didn't dispute the dire prediction. Depressingly, neither did Porter Hubbard.

8

THERE were flickering signs of hope the next morning; indications that the human spirit and reason still flourished in Barfield. The head nurse on the morning shift reported that her brother, editor of the *Register*, had handed in his resignation, protesting against the slanted news story.

"Mr. Barfield had one of his toadies write it," the head nurse said. "My brother objected, but the publisher went over his head, so Bruce up and quit."

"What will he do now?" Ellen asked. "There isn't another editorial job in this town. Only one newspaper."

The head nurse shrugged. "There's only one hospital, too. But if they force Dr. Sterling out of here . . . " (she thumbed towards a room next to Administration office, where the

111

Hospital Board was in session) " . . . I'll quit, too."

This was one of the employees Jerry Sterling had accused of working only for a salary; one of the people who 'didn't care'!

Her brother might seek employment at the local radio station, she said; it was an operation independent of Henry Barfield's financial interest. "At least they're reporting the truth. Did you hear the newscast this morning?"

Ellen hadn't, but just hearing about a man who placed integrity before security, and of a communications media that recognised its responsibility to the public, rekindled her faith in the existence of David's 'good people'.

At ten-fifteen that faith was buoyed again. Joan Eliot's father appeared at the nurses' station, giving a twofold reason for his presence. First, he wanted to talk to Dr. Sterling about a stronger liaison between the college and the hospital. "I'm heading a faculty committee organised to set up a student health service," Mr. Eliot said. "We don't even know where to begin. I'm sure Dr. Sterling will be an invaluable aid to us."

Mr. Eliot's second reason for coming was more ambiguous. He had been troubled by shoulder pains that 'might be bursitis'; he wanted Dr. Sterling to examine him.

Ellen sensed that the latter reason, at least, was an invention. Mr Eliot had read between the lines in this morning's paper. He had come to lend his weight, as a respected member of the community, in a fight for justice. What better way to demonstrate his faith in Jerry Sterling than to submit himself as a patient?

"I'll tell the doctor you're here," Ellen said. She resisted the urge to say, "Thank you for coming."

Three encouraging bits to report to Jerry! He had deserted his office, staying far away from the room in which the Hospital Board was weighing his future. Ellen found him checking through the files in the X-ray department.

He only nodded vaguely at Ellen's brief reports about the newspaper editor, the unbiased radio station; Jerry despised petty gossip, and he seemed to view even these optimistic personal notes as demeaning. His attitude seemed to be that a just man didn't need defenders; his course was right and his conscience was clear. Nothing else seemed relevant.

Ellen cut the encouraging news short, her own enthusiasm suddenly dampened. The doctor was looking at her expectantly, as though he were wondering why she had interrupted his work.

"Mr. Eliot's waiting to see you in the reception room, Doctor. You remember him — you treated his daughter, Joan?"

Jerry released a soft sigh. "Did he tell you what his complaint is?"

"He thinks it's bursitis," Ellen said.

"No, no. I meant . . . " Jerry ran the heel of his hand over his forehead. "That's paranoia for you, Miss Whitaker. By 'complaint' I assumed he had jumped on the bandwagon."

"On the contrary. He wants to get your advice about setting up a health service for the college."

For an instant, the coal black eyes lighted with interest. Then, as abruptly, Jerry Sterling's face clouded. He sounded like a man who no longer dared to permit himself to get excited about a new project. "I'll talk to him, of course. Give him what suggestions I can. I'll have to explain to him, though, that . . . I won't be here to give him any physical co-operation."

Ellen's legs threatened to give in under her. "You won't . . . ?"

"I shouldn't be jumping the gun before I give my resignation to the Board. It seems fair to give you warning, Miss Whitaker. You've . . . " Jerry hesitated, his gaze unable to meet Ellen's. " . . . You've pretty much gone out on a limb for me. You'll only inherit some of my problems if you stay. So . . . you might want to start thinking about . . . another job elsewhere." He glanced upwards, forcing himself to face Ellen. "I'm sorry. I'm truly sorry."

"You *can't* give up!" Ellen cried. "I just tried to tell you — there *are* people who . . . "

"If I had no one but myself to think about, I'd hold my ground until hell freezes over," Jerry said. "I'd let them try to force me out, and fight it legally — every way I know how."

"Then . . . "

"Enough people have suffered because they stood by me." Jerry had walked to the door, standing there with his back to Ellen, obviously struggling to keep his voice steady. "Porter Hubbard's neglected his business until it's a shambles, out beating the drums for me. My folks had to leave a town they'd grown up in — start all over in their sixties, among strangers. You tell me about a man who quit his job today . . . "

"Don't feel sorry for people who have principles," Ellen pleaded. "Feel sorry for . . . "

"For a young doctor who's trying to make a niche for himself? A doctor they're going to smear, right along with me, because he was assisting when that child died on my operating table? This town needs Dr. Grath. It needs half a dozen more like him. They won't come, Miss Whitaker. As long as this place is a battlefield instead of a hospital, they won't come to Barfield. And Dr. Grath's going to go down with the ruins."

Ellen dredged her mind for a strong argument. "He's already on Henry Barfield's revenge list. Are you going to walk out and let him fight it out alone?"

"He'll build a practice once he's disassociated himself from me." Jerry turned around, and it seemed that all the pain in the world was distilled in his eyes. "It's the *hospital*, Miss Whitaker. I can't go on standing between thousands

117

of people and their hospital."

"But they don't understand! We've got to . . . "

"I haven't made this decision lightly," Jerry said. It was the most agonising understatement Ellen had ever heard. "There are other doctors for this place. Other places for me."

He was gone then, walking towards his meeting with Mr. Eliot with exaggeratedly buoyant steps, pretending that he hadn't made the most excruciating decision of his life. Or that giving up the challenge and the dream of Barfield Hospital, leaving the town without clearing his name, was not as important as his immediate mission.

For weeks the explosion had been building inside Ellen. She watched Jerry's pseudo-brave stride down the corridor, seeing him raise his head a little higher as he passed the meeting room. The gesture was all that was needed to trigger Ellen's suppressed fury. *My father would have done this, she thought. He wouldn't have cared about the consequences. He'd have had the satisfaction of telling those vultures what he thinks of them*!

She didn't remember racing down the hall or flinging the door open. She was there, facing the startled group of men seated around the conference table, just as she had faced the gossips in her mother's dining room.

"I hope you're satisfied! You don't have to waste any more time trying to find ways to crucify Dr. Sterling. He's written his resignation. You've broken him and he's leaving!" Ellen's cries filled the room and she ignored the tears that raced down her cheeks. "I'm sorry for everyone in this town. But I'm glad too. You didn't deserve him. You had a doctor who cared . . . "

"Miss Whitaker!"

" . . . and you didn't deserve him!"

"Miss Whitaker!" Henry Barfield was on his feet, his hound-dog features red with anger.

Porter had risen, too, from his place

at the head of the table. "Ellen, this isn't the way."

"Then go on buttering them up, smoothing over their lies. They're vicious, vindictive, heartless . . . "

"I won't listen to this," Henry shrilled. "A nurse, breaking in here like this! I demand that she be dismissed!"

Words no longer mattered. Ellen was sobbing, looking from one shocked face to another, seeing two men she hadn't seen entering the hospital this morning: the local sheriff and Dr. Vosbergh. "What are you going to do — accuse him of murder? No doctor's ever fought harder to save a patient! You watched him work, Dr. Vosbergh!" She turned towards the elderly doctor, seeing his face redden at the mention of his name. "Why did you walk out on him? So that you could help these hypocrites plan for the day when you'd take over Dr. Sterling's job?"

Porter Hubbard's voice, usually low

and gentle, cracked across the room like a bullwhip. "Sheriff Garvey came here at my request."

Ellen sucked in a sharp breath. "You . . . "

"First, to remind these gentlemen that there was no possibility that Dr. Sterling was involved in his wife's death. To bury that rumour, once and for all. And, second, to tell us he's started an investigation of that cult the Eldridges belong to. Following up Dr. Sterling's charge of child neglect."

The room threatened to close down over Ellen's head. "I . . . I didn't know that. I'm . . . "

"Dr. Vosbergh left his sickbed at home, against Dr. Grath's orders. He came to substantiate the charge. To tell us about other cases he's seen from the colony. Old people whose health had been jeopardised by fanatical fasting. When you broke into the room, he was telling us that that phoney 'Deacon' is attracting new disciples with a phoney 'Spiritual cancer cure'.

Herb teas he's 'blessed' . . . practicing medicine without a licence."

Ellen reached out for the back of a chair to steady herself. "The others. You said — Mr. Barfield would come armed with . . . "

"Facts and figures," Henry shouted. "I'm going to add another charge to my dossier . . . " He pounded his fist on a leather portfolio before him on the table. "Dr. Sterling isn't qualified to hire personnel for this hospital. I think these gentlemen have just seen that for themselves."

Porter's tone dropped to its normal low register. "I think the rabble-rousing idea your brother had was better than this, Ellen. Now, if you'll . . . excuse us?"

She heard the same defeat in Porter's voice that she had heard in Jerry's. Her choking apology was meaningless. Ellen spun around and hurried out of the room, unable to control her sobs. Someone else closed the door quietly behind her.

She managed, somehow, to get through the day, conscious of the fact that she had ruined Porter Hubbard's carefully planned attempt to restore reason. Worse, there was no doubt that her insane outburst had carried to the reception rooms.

Long after the meeting had adjourned, before she escaped for home at three o'clock, Ellen made a second shame-faced apology to Jerry Sterling.

He was not vindictive only sorrowful as he said, "I had enough stacked against me without the Board thinking I hired you for . . . personal reasons."

He left the rest unsaid, but Ellen could see and hear the scene she had created through the suspicious eyes and ears of Henry Barfield's supporters. Only a woman in love with a man would defend him like a wildcat. Only a doctor in love with her would hire a nurse so completely unable to control her emotions. An imagined love affair — perhaps of long duration — might provide another motive, besides money, for a man to want his wife out of the way.

Jerry Sterling didn't dredge up the old ghosts. He merely closed his eyes for a moment, murmuring, "I would have liked to bow out with the only thing I had left. A little dignity."

9

"THIS is what you needed," Joan Eliot said.

She sat between David and Ellen in the front seat of David's old sedan. They had been driving along the mountain road towards Templeton for the last half hour, both of the younger people working hard to raise Ellen's depressed spirits.

From behind the wheel, David said, "Yah, you get out here and dig this terrific scenery, get a whiff of this clean air, and things don't look so dismal."

If Joan had ever had psychic talents, cracking her head on a swimming pool floor had not curtailed them. "What your sister needs, Dave," she said. " . . . what she really needs is a good, stiff drink."

"I don't . . . !"

Ellen's protest was ignored. "Okay,

then. A not-so-stiff beer. The Tumble-weed Inn's just up the road, Dave. Let's stop there, huh?"

David manoeuvred a sharp turn, exposing a breath-taking view of purple-blue mountains ridged by shadow and light, touched with gold by the setting sun. "I brought you out to see *this*, not to sit in that crumby place. Smoke, stale beer smell . . . "

"This early, there won't be a soul there except that poker-faced bartender," Joan insisted. "I think he owns the place."

"Joanie's fascinated by ex-hoodlums," David said. "She'd have had a ball in Chicago during the twenties."

"I'm going to be a sociology major," Joan pointed out smugly. "So what's wrong with studying the seamy side of life?"

"Nothing. Just . . . study it out of books," David said. For someone who had suggested this ride as a means of cheering up his sister, he sounded inordinately grim. He didn't even turn his head, minutes later, when they reached a plateau and passed The Tumbleweed Inn.

It was a rundown frame building, box-shaped, that in a bygone era would have been referred to as a 'roadhouse'. An unlighted neon sigh promised BEER, EATS AND DANCING.

"You're right," Joan agreed. "It looks seedier than I remembered. Gee, I haven't been up here in ages."

"It always *was* a shoddy place," David told her. "You didn't notice it because it was a kick to come up here when we were in high school. It was sort of a defiance thing. Like, everybody's folks would have had a fit if they knew we drove up here on Saturday nights. All we did was sneak a few beers and dance to the jukebox, but it was considered a big deal."

"Forbidden fruit. You outgrow that immature kind of rebellion," Joan said.

Except for her depression, Ellen would have smiled at this naïve wisdom.

"I guess I decided it wasn't for me when I heard about that quack doctor who used to hang around the place," Joan continued.

"Not 'Deacon Justice'?" Ellen exclaimed.

"Oh, no! This was a real doctor. Some sad alcoholic who lost his licence to practice. What was his name, Dave? Dr. Webberly . . . Wibberly, something like that. I only saw him there once, so drunk he couldn't stand up. Then a girl I used to know told me he made his living doing . . . you know. *Those* kind of operations."

"Will you cut it out?" David cried. "Who cares about some old drunk?"

"I was *only* saying," Joan persisted, "why I wouldn't let a date take me there anymore. I mean, that's all my dad had to know about the place. He'd have pounded my head in if he'd found out." Joan sighed a world-weary sigh. "It was seamy, all right. In fact the poor old drunk committed suicide. Right after that awful thing

128

with Naomi. If you ask me, the sheriff suspected, and *I* suspected . . . "

"*I said will you cool it?*" David's voice had risen to a strident pitch, and the old car lurched forward as he pressed his foot against the accelerator.

Joan was silent until he started to pull into the driveway of a mountain cabin.

"Don't let's go back the way we came," Joan said. "Go straight ahead."

"It's longer going the circle route," David told her.

"I know, but it's flatter. It's getting dark." She turned to Ellen. "I have a thing about driving on rim roads after dark. Please make him go back the easy way."

"We aren't in a hurry," Ellen said. Her mind was churning and she dreaded an argument. "I get nervous on rim roads, too, when I can't see the edge."

David grumbled something under his breath and continued on the circular road that would take them through

Templeton and back to Barfield.

About twenty minutes later, with the conversation turned to more agreeable subjects, the headlights caught a thick clump of scraggly bushes bordering the roadside.

"I always feel cold chills when I pass this spot," Joan said. In the cramped front seat, Ellen felt the shudder of the girl's body against her own. "That's where they found Naomi's body, you know. In a ditch, under those bushes."

There was no comment from David, but Ellen's heart stopped for a moment as she glanced in his direction. The sun had set, and he had turned the lights on soon after they passed the tavern and motel at the summit. Now, in the faint glow from the dashboard, David's face reflected a sickly pallor. His jaw was set in a determined line, and he clutched the steering wheel like someone drowning.

"Nobody likes to talk about it," Joan said in a funereal tone. "All of us kids — we went to grade school together, and then high school. Naomi was prom queen. Everybody thought she'd make it big in New York or Hollywood. Nobody every dreamed she'd come back here and settle down, married to a doctor."

Sometime during her nostalgic reminiscence, Joan had started to cry; quietly, apparently unaware of the huge, rolling tears. "Lorna says she was a tramp, but I don't like to remember her that way. Before they built the junior college, when my dad was still teaching at the high school, she used to come over and we'd talk. About how neat her grandfather was, and how she hated her Uncle Henry and her Aunt Carrie because they hated her. And how much she wanted somebody to love her. Her mother and dad never cared. They were always off somewhere, leaving her alone with her grandfather. She couldn't get enough love. She grabbed it from everybody. Her cousin Lorna, Dave, me, all the kids at school. Everybody."

"Everybody liked her," Ellen remembered.

Joan blinked at her tears. "You mean she was popular. Sure. She had looks, she had a convertible, she had nice clothes, she used to laugh a lot. A party didn't swing until Naomi got there. But she was never sure anybody liked *her*. Like, if she *hadn't* been named Barfield, and if she *didn't* have so many things going for her."

"It's cold out tonight," David said. "Funny, this close to June, it's usually warmer."

Joan didn't respond to the pointed interruption. "I guess she thought she'd have everybody crazy about her if she made it as an actress. But she was a flop there. She wasn't like Lorna — Lorna has talent. She'll probably bring the house down at the one-act play competition in Denver next week."

"I'd like to go," David said. "What say we all go?"

"Then, when Naomi came back, and

somebody *really* fell head over heels in love with her — or maybe Dr. Sterling always felt that way, I don't know. Anyway, I figured, 'This is it. It's all Naomi ever needed,'" Joan was thoughtful for a moment. "It wasn't, though. I guess Naomi wanted all the love in the world. She had to win over every man who appealed to her. Old boy friends, new fellows in town. Naomi couldn't let *anybody* go."

"I used to envy her," Ellen recalled. "I was so jealous . . . "

"*Jealous*? I was one of her best friends," Joan said. "And I'd go to bed at night wishing she was dead. Like, when *you* were dating her, Dave. In our senior year. I saw you smooching with her on the dance floor one night in The Tumbleweed, and I wanted to scratch her eyes out."

"Long time ago," David said tersely. "Forget it."

"David? I didn't know you'd ever dated Naomi," Ellen said. "I was gone when you were a senior, but . . . "

"Forget it!" David cried. *"Will you just plain drop the subject!"*

Joan offered a pacifying remark. "That wasn't unusual. Just about every attractive guy in town dated Naomi at one time or another. Even after she married. And everybody knew it, too, except Dr. Sterling."

David was speeding towards Barfield as though the devil sat on his rear bumper. "That's why you can't blame people for thinking the way they do," he said. "When he found out — I guess he had a good motive to kill her. Understand, I'm not implying that he *did*."

Nearer to town, David was able to get radio reception. They drove towards the lights of Barfield saying nothing, listening to the local station's collection of old Bing Crosby records.

Nightmare piled upon nightmare, Ellen thought. David's refusal to stop at The Tumbleweed, his nervousness as Joan talked about the old rendezvous place and the alcoholic ex-doctor who had killed himself soon after Naomi's death. Then, David's reluctance to drive by the spot where Naomi's body had been found, and his edgy reaction when Joan mentioned his dates with the girl Jerry Sterling had married.

Bored with her life as a small-town doctor's wife Naomi had dated 'every man who appealed to her'. '*Her old boyfriends*,' Joan had said!

David had never mentioned his dates with Naomi. Why hadn't he. *Because he was one of the old loves she had turned back to in her insatiable quest for love?*

If not, why the uneasiness, why the attempts to silence Joan, why the agitated expression on David's face *now?*

It's too much, Ellen thought desperately. Jerry, the gossips, the pressures, the death of that pathetic little boy. *Me, losing my head and making a fool of myself, alienating Jerry for all time. Too much!*

Yet, all of it was bearable except the

terrifying thought that Jerry Sterling might be cleared of suspicion. Exonerated, as Peter Hubbard had said, 'once and for all'. Cleared, reinstated, justified — and respected again. But at what price to Ellen's own brother?

10

PORTER HUBBARD was not long in forgiving Ellen's behaviour before the Hospital Board. It hadn't helped, he admitted, but she had acted out of righteous indignation. Besides, it didn't matter now. Jerry Sterling was adamant about leaving Barfield.

"I'm sorry to see Jerry quitting just as I felt we were making some progress," Porter said. "I just left the hospital. He's working late, getting all the records in order to . . . turn over to his successor."

They were sitting in the Whitaker's breakfast nook, lingering over coffee. A chilly rain pelted the window, adding to the gloomy atmosphere.

Ellen stared into the dregs of her cup. "Have they chosen a replacement, yet?"

"No. That'll take time. A G.P. who specialises in surgery and knows administration . . . one who's willing to settle in an isolated small town and work for the kind of salary Jerry's been living on . . . " Porter made a hopeless gesture. "They don't grow on trees, do they? Neither do surgical nurses who can fill in wherever they're needed."

"Porter, you promised me we wouldn't talk about that any more."

"You're really determined to go?"

"I've already written a letter to my old supervisor in Chicago," Ellen told him. "Let's see . . . this is Saturday night. If I get it in the mail — air mail — tomorrow, I should be getting an answer by the end of next week. I know the job's waiting. I'm almost packed."

"I wish you'd come with me tonight," Porter said. He shot a swift glance at his watch. "At least don't leave thinking everybody in Barfield is a monster."

"David asked me to go, too," Ellen said. "He and Joan had planned to go

138

all the way to Denver for that drama festival, but Mom needed him at the dinner house yesterday. So the kids settled for going to the welcoming party at the college."

"Not bad for a provincial burg like this." Porter beamed his civic pride. "Second prize in the one-act play contest, and — I guess you heard it on the radio — three awards for individual performances. They're going to get a real brass band homecoming when that bus pulls up in front of the auditorium."

"It's going on nine," Ellen reminded him. She wanted nothing more than to be alone — the way Jerry Sterling was alone tonight, getting ready to turn his dream over to a stranger. "Isn't the bus due in at nine-thirty? You don't want to be late."

"No, but . . . I want you to come with me," Porter urged. "I want you to see the wonderful spirit. The friendliness — the co-operation. For a few hours, all the factions bury the hatchet to show our young people we're proud of them. They cheer *losers*, too. Why, the year our high-school team came in next to bottom in the county basketball league, we threw a better-luck-next-time dance for them! Tonight, you'll get a whole new concept of . . ."

"Excuse me, Porter." Ellen reached over to a kitchen counter to answer the interrupting telephone. "This will be for David. It always is."

It wasn't a call for David. Ellen's hand tightened on the receiver the instant she heard the voice of the night-shift nurse. Listening, she felt the blood drain from her face; the sudden furious pounding of her heart. The message was brief. Ellen responded with only two words: "Right away."

She was on her feet, hurrying towards the door. "You've got to drive me past the hospital to pick up first-aid supplies and . . ."

Porter was behind her. "What is it? What happened?" Porter's Lincoln was parked at the kerb. "The chartered bus. A truck driver saw it skid through a mud slide and go over the embankment, five miles out on the Templeton road."

"My God! Did he . . . ?"

"He didn't stop. He did the sensible thing — rushed into town and called the hospital."

★ ★ ★

Like all bad news, word had raced through Barfield like quicksilver. Apparently everyone who had been assembled at the college auditorium was headed for the accident site. By the time Ellen had picked up the kit waiting for her in the Emergency Room, cars were crawling like ants on the mountain highway, impeding the arrival of medical help. The town's lone ambulance had already been dispatched; through the rain, Ellen spotted a hearse, which had been pressed into ambulance duty, trying to honk its way through the obstructing cavalcade of curiosity seekers and anxious relatives.

Brilliant lights from two sheriff's cars and a tow truck illuminated the crowded, muddy road at the scene of the accident. Officers, firemen and a volunteer group of citizens worked frantically to clear the way for the arriving doctors and nurses, pleading with people to leave, to move their cars out of the way, to stand away from the embankment so that the injured could be brought up the clay-slicked bank.

Some twenty feet below the side of the road, spotlights were trained on the bus itself. Its front end smashed, it lay on its side like a gigantic dying animal. It had come to a crashing stop on a rocky ledge, only inches away from a barely visible drop-off point. At this elevation, the chasm beyond it probably dropped six or seven hundred feet. Around the big yellow vehicle, strewn about like limp rag dolls, Ellen saw the pride and joy of Barfield . . . the college drama class they had gathered to honour this evening.

Among the still figures, and those who sat up, bleeding and dazed, Ellen spotted Jerry Sterling and Dr. Grath. Several nurses had arrived before her. Astoundingly, Dr. Vosbergh, looking far from well, was puffing his way through the crowd on the road, crying, "Let me through! I'm a doctor . . . let me get through!"

Ellen felt a quick squeeze of Porter's hand on her arm. "Be careful down there. It's slippery and you'll be close to the edge . . . "

Gripping the black emergency kit by its handle, Ellen shoved aside a group of gaping spectators and let herself down over the steep roadside. Scrub bush and rocks scraped her legs as she slid the last few feet of the way down to the ledge. Behind her, over the insistent patter of the rain, she heard a male voice booming over a loudspeaker, "Folks, please! We've got to clear the way for the ambulances to leave! Will everyone except medical personnel please move your cars. Let's give those injured kids a chance . . . "

Jerry Sterling had taken command. Mud-splattered, his suit dripping wet, he seemed to be everywhere at once, directing emergency treatment, giving commands with a firmly controlled voice, interrupting his orders to give emergency treatment to one of the victims who had been extracted from the bus, answering questions unhesitatingly.

One ambulance, one hearse, several station wagons. And not one of the twenty or more occupants of the bus who had escaped some injury! An ambulance attendant slipped, falling near Ellen, then struggled back to his feet, shouting, "Who goes first, Doctor!"

Jerry had made his decisions . . . decisions involving awesome responsibility. While Ellen gave first aid to a girl who kept sobbing, "Help me! oh, somebody, please help me!" two stretchers moved tortuously up the slippery embankment.

One of them bore the young man Ellen had tended first. The other, seen only dimly as the cliff blotted out the searchlights, carried Lorna Barfield.

"They'll be back for you as fast as they can," a tired old voice kept repeating. "You'll all get help . . . try to stay calm. Stay calm." It was Dr. Vosbergh's voice. While he talked, he was treating an unconscious girl whose forehead and cheek had taken the brunt of glass from a shattered window.

"Miss Whitaker, I want you to come with me." That was Dr. Sterling's voice. "Dr. Grath will stay here with four nurses. The rest of us are going back to Surgery on the first trip. We'll be set as the patients arrive."

He was helping Ellen up the muddy slope, then. And boosting her up over the top, to drop down again, this time lending his shoulder to the full weight of Dr. Vosbergh. Breathing hard, looking paler than most of the patients he had been working over, the old doctor reached the road with difficulty. One of his hands clutched at his left upper arm.

"Dr. Vosbergh, I think you had better . . . "

Jerry's concern was waved away. "I'll be all right. Just . . . out of breath."

Following the ambulance attendants, Ellen was aware of Carrie Barfield's hysterical sobs. "Lorna . . . my baby . . . oh, Lorna!" Henry Barfield was at his wife's side, his arm around her heaving shoulders. "She'll be all right, Carrie. She's got to be all right."

Sounds of rain, hollow cries rising from the victims still left behind, agonised questions from the crowd of parents and friends. Then, louder than the others, a shaking male voice demanding, "Where are you taking my boy? You're not taking him to Barfield! Turn that killer loose on him, like that little Eldridge kid? No, you don't! He's going to Templeton!"

Ellen spun around to see the fear-crazed face of a thin, middle-aged man. She had seen him around town wearing overalls. Tonight he was dressed in an ill-fitting brown suit; obviously he had been part of the proud welcoming crowd.

Porter was trying to calm the man. "Bill, your boy's badly hurt. Time the ambulances from Templeton get here . . . "

"Take him there!" the man cried. "Take him to a good doctor in . . . "

"The road's slick from mud slides all across the pass!"

"Take the long road, then! Go through town! He's my kid — you aren't taking him to that butcher shop!"

The man had placed himself between the ambulance and the stretcher, blocking passage for the litters carrying his son and Lorna Barfield.

"Mr. Barfield, back me up! You've got influence! Tell them! You know what that hospital will do to our kids. Your own daughter — *tell them what you told me about that doctor, there!*"

"*You damned fool!*" Dr. Vosbergh

had elbowed his way into the foreground. His huge body trembled with the force of his cry. "Dr. Sterling's sending these two first because they're haemorrhaging internally. If they don't get to an operating room fast, by the time you get them to Templeton, they'll both be dead!"

Carrie Barfield shrieked, "No! Oh, no, no, no . . . "

"Henry, tell them the truth. I delivered Lorna! Every second we waste here . . . " Dr. Vosbergh gasped, his hands flying to his chest. Ellen moved swiftly to give him support. He forced himself to stand upright, gasping for breath. "I'm all right, girl. Tell him . . . Henry, tell him . . . there isn't a . . . better doctor . . . anywhere!"

For a terrible instant Henry Barfield looked from Dr. Vosbergh to Jerry Sterling, and then to the still form of his daughter. A widening pool of blood stained the blanket that covered her body. From beneath the blanket, a shoeless foot protruded. Grotesquely, the other foot still wore a beige high-heeled pump; one of the new shoes Lorna had chosen to match the pretty frock she had worn to her triumph in Denver.

"Henry . . . she's going to die! I . . . I can't help her! Are you going to kill her with the poison you've spread through the town?"

The frozen tableau could not have taken more than five seconds. Yet it seemed to Ellen that an eternity had gone by before Henry Barfield moved. Grabbing the other terror-stricken father's arm, he said, "Get out of the way, Bill." The words emerged more like a sob than a command. "My father left this hospital for this. He left a . . . doctor, too."

Dazed, the other man let himself be led out of the way. Porter was reassuring all three of the parents as the two stretchers were eased into the ambulance. Other victims, less seriously injured, were being carried up from the disaster site to other conveyances as Ellen joined Jerry Sterling in the two seats next to Lorna and the other patient.

Firemen and the sheriff's deputies had cleared a path in the road towards Barfield Hospital. Lorna Barfield's father had cleared another.

11

IT was not over. Numb with fatigue, Ellen flashed a glance at the clock on the O.R. wall. 4.20 a.m. It was easier now, with Dr. Grath supervising activity in the Emergency Room. At three o'clock, he had released one of the nurses, giving the surgical team one more pair of hands.

Jerry Sterling finished the closure on an injury that had required probing out glass, debridement, and extensive suturing. It was Emergency Room work, comparatively minor after the jobs that had occupied him throughout the long night.

He stepped back as the relief nurse moved up to apply dressings. His sigh might have come from a wind tunnel. "What's next?"

"Nothing more here, Doctor," Ellen said.

"I'm going over to see if Dr. Grath needs a hand. I suppose you're ready to drop?"

"I'm fine," Ellen assured him. "After we get this patient to Recovery, I'll . . . "

"I think Dr. Grath has everything under control." the other nurse said.

"We'll check," Jerry muttered. "If that's the case, you and Miss Llewelyn had better stay in Recovery. Call me if there's any change."

He was referring to the two major surgical cases he had taken care of first. Eons ago, it seemed to Ellen. A splenectomy, and resection of the small intestine had been required by the young male patient. Lorna Barfield's injuries had required more extensive surgery. Twice, during the two-hour-long operation, Miss Llewelyn had called for additional units of whole blood. Jerry Sterling had laboured in quiet desperation, detaining Dr. Grath as his assistant only as long as four hands were needed, then turning from the operating table to determine where he was needed next.

Shortly after sunrise, with the help of two nurses who had not been located during the height of the emergency. Jerry made certain that the fourteen patients newly admitted to Barfield Hospital were receiving proper medication. Saline, whole blood, antibiotics poured into the veins of surgical cases and shock victims. Eight patients had been given first-aid care and dismissed. Thus far, there had been one fatality; the driver of the bus had been pronounced dead at the scene of the accident. Two cases were listed as serious; Lorna Barfield's condition was considered critical.

Lorna's parents were in the reception room when Ellen urged Jerry Sterling and Dr. Grath to take a few minutes out for coffee. Carrie Barfield didn't move from the settee where she had evidently been sitting all night. Her neon-bright red hair looked damp and dishevelled; her eyes, puffy and discoloured, remained closed, as if in prayer.

It was her husband who crossed the room to the coffee machine around which Ellen and the doctors were clustered. The drooping lines of his face looked more haggard than ever. "Jerry . . . " It was no more than a croaking sound. "Jerry, I don't know . . . "

Jerry spared him the pain of an apology. "She's holding her own, Henry. We've got through the most critical hours. Go home and try to get some sleep."

"I couldn't go home," Henry muttered. "Carrie and I . . . "

"Stretch out here in the reception room, then," Jerry said. "I'll see that Carrie gets some sedatives."

"Jerry . . . " Henry's voice failed him. He turned away, speechless, blinking back tears.

Jerry forgot about the paper cup in his hand. He carried it to the window, addressing a third member of the 'welcoming party' Ellen had not noticed before; the man Porter had called Bill. "Your boy is doing better than we expected," Jerry said. "He's resting quietly. Come back later and you'll be able to see him in his room."

The man nodded dumbly. He stared at 'the killer' with uncomprehending eyes. "You sure? I don't have anybody else. Don't tell me a thing like that if . . . "

Jerry patted the man's back lightly with his free hand. "I'm sure," he said.

Dr. Grath drained the last of his coffee. "I'd better get back," he said. "I want to tell you first, Jerry . . . if you hadn't done an administrative job the likes of which I've never seen before . . . "

"Get back to where?" Jerry asked. "Look, there's nothing to do in emergency. Why don't you sack out for a few hours?"

Dr. Grath removed his glasses, blew

a cloud of steam at the lenses, and wiped them off with a pad of gauze he extracted from his white jacket. "I left Miss Harkness with Dr. Vosbergh. I expect she could use some relief."

Dr. Vosbergh! Ellen had been too busy to wonder about the absence of the old doctor. Apparently Jerry hadn't had time to miss him, either. "I didn't know . . ."

"He collapsed, just as we were getting our last patient into the ambulance," Dr. Grath said. "It was too much for him." Among his many other duties during the night, it developed that the new doctor in town had been ministering to the victim of a heart attack. "I've done everything I can, Jerry. You might want to check — Room 108."

"Let me go, Vernon," Jerry said. "Go lie down. We can't afford another collapse."

Ellen was hurrying down the corridor after Jerry Sterling, trying to keep up with his rapid stride, when Miss

Harkness emerged from Room 108. "Doctor — I was coming out to call you."

"What is it?"

"Dr. Vosbergh wants to see you. I'm afraid he's . . . "

Jerry brushed past the elderly nurse. He indicated that he wanted Ellen to follow him.

It was daylight outside and the rain had stopped falling, but the draperies had been drawn; only a shaded light on the night stand illuminated the room. Ellen closed the door behind her quietly.

Dr. Vosbergh was propped up in a semi-reclining position, the hospital bed raised under his head. An ice bag sat askew over his grey hair, giving the beefy red face an incongruously rakish appearance. His breath seemed laboured; an oxygen mask waited in readiness above his bed.

"You shouldn't have come out tonight," Jerry accused softly. "Doing any better now?"

Ellen waited back in the shadows of the room, barely able to stand on her feet. Dr. Vosbergh shook his leonine head back and forth slowly. "I have to . . . talk to you, Jerry. Something I . . . have to tell you."

"I'd rather it waited," Jerry said. "Whatever it is will keep until you're feeling stronger. I want you to rest."

"I can't . . . risk that," Dr. Vosbergh said. "You can't fool an old . . . war-horse like me — you young doctors. Not dry behind the ears yet." He made a grim face that was undoubtedly intended as a smile. "Listen to me, Jerry. While I'm still here . . . let me tell you. Let me get it off my conscience."

He spoke slowly, with tremendous effort, but Dr. Vosbergh seemed to be forcing the words out as if someone were holding a stop watch over him. "Naomi came to me. I brought her into this world, Jerry . . . I was always there when she . . . needed help."

Jerry's face had frozen into grim,

expectant lines. "I know that. You were always . . ."

"No, wait. Hear me out. When she was in trouble . . . she came to me. She asked me to do . . . what I couldn't do, Jerry. She cried like a baby and I . . . I had all I could do to tell her . . . I couldn't help her."

Neither Dr. Vosbergh nor Jerry seemed aware of Ellen's presence. She debated about slipping out of the room, then found herself glued to the spot by the old doctor's fading voice.

"I should have known . . . I was turning her over to a drunken quack . . . to a butcher. And I let her go, Jerry." Dr. Vosbergh's voice rose to an agitated pitch. "I let her walk out of my office to her death."

"Easy," Jerry murmured. "You did the only thing you could do. Don't bother yourself with it, Doctor. I would have done . . ."

"*Why didn't you?*" Dr. Vosbergh cried out. "I wouldn't have let her go, knowing the . . . state she was in. Or . . . then . . . I would have talked to you . . . except that she told me . . . at the end . . . when I told her I couldn't, I . . . I wouldn't . . . "

Jerry leaned forward, towards the bed. "Tomorrow, Doctor. We'll talk about it tomorrow."

"No. No, I may not . . . " Dr. Vosbergh drew a wheezing breath. "Let me tell you this now, so I can . . . rest. I've had Naomi on my conscience all this time. But I've wondered . . . why didn't *you* help her? Ethics . . . you wouldn't have let her go to a quack because of . . . ethics. I *said* you'd help her . . . I would have talked to you, otherwise. We'd have . . . found some way to . . . "

"She didn't tell me," Jerry whispered. "I didn't know she was expecting a baby until . . . they came to tell me she was dead."

Dr. Vosbergh stared at him for a long while. "She said I wasn't to . . . worry. That's the last thing she said to me,

Jerry. She said . . . 'Forget I talked to you, Doctor. I'll talk to Hubby. He'll know what to do.'"

Jerry's body stiffened. "She said . . . "

"I told her . . . yes — yes, that was the right thing to do. Tell your husband. He loves you. He's a doctor. He'll . . . " Dr. Vosbergh, raised his head from the pillow. "I know you didn't do it, Jerry! But why did you let her go to someone else?"

Jerry's hand reached out, returning the older doctor to a relaxed position. "I didn't know. She must have decided not to tell me. Sleep, now. Try to sleep."

Dr. Vosbergh's eyes had closed, and Ellen stepped forward, assuming the worst.

Jerry motioned her back, lingering for another minute over the reclining figure. After a while he said, "He's asleep." Jerry circled the bed to check the chart posted at the foot. "Good. Shouldn't have let him fight off sedation that long."

He signalled to Ellen, and together they left the room.

In the corridor, outside the door, Jerry stopped. He was exhausted, Ellen knew. Completely worn out. But why didn't he find somewhere to lie down, instead of covering his face with his hands, pressing his fingers against his eye sockets like someone trying to blot out an unbearable horror?

"Doctor . . . ?"

He dropped his hands to his side. "Did you hear him, Ellen. Did you hear him say . . . ?"

"I'm sorry," Ellen told him. "I didn't want to . . . eavesdrop on your personal life."

Jerry hadn't heard her apology. He was staring past Ellen, staring vacantly down the corridor into space, into a still unburied past. "She never called me 'Hubby'." he said slowly. "Naomi had a pet name for everybody. I was 'Jer', 'honey', 'doc' . . . 'Hubby'. *Hubby!* That was the name she used for Porter Hubbard."

12

D R. VOSBERGH'S prognosis for himself turned out to be erroneous. When he had summoned Jerry Sterling into his room on the night of the bus disaster, he had evidently thought he was making a deathbed confession. He had been wrong.

There was no longer any doubt that he had limited his patient load because of a threatening heart condition, and not because he had joined the boycott against Jerry Sterling. But the cardiac problem, aggravated by his excitement and physical stress, responded to expert care. Dr. Vosbergh was far from being a well man, but ten days after his collapse he was ready to be released from Barfield Hospital.

"These young doctors," he complained to Ellen. "Telling me I've got to take it easy." He winked. "It's all a plot to take over my practice."

"I hear Dr. Grath's going to do that," Ellen said. "I've also heard that it was your idea, Doctor. You aren't the only one who's deserting us this week, you know."

He nodded. "I know. They've got Lorna up — she stopped in to see me this morning. And Bill Masterson's boy. No — he went home yesterday, didn't he? I simply don't understand it. Here Porter Hubbard, and the Eliots, and I don't know how many others are going around getting signatures on a petition, asking Dr. Sterling to stay. The paper ran that big editorial on the front page last week . . . about the debt of gratitude Barfield owed to its doctors. It was so mushy, it was almost embarrassing to read it, but everything Henry wrote about this hospital is true."

"Including the fact that it's managed on a shamefully skimpy budget," Ellen pointed out. "We were lucky to be prepared for that accident, weren't we? Imagine a major disaster, though. As short-handed as we were."

"There'll have to be an increased staff, now that admissions are going up," Dr. Vosbergh said. "And an outpouring of money for equipment. I may be talking out of turn, but Porter tells me the Barfields are going to get Jerry Sterling's inheritance out of the courts and into his pocket. I don't have to tell you where he'll spend it."

"He never wanted that money for himself," Ellen said. "I'm sure it has . . . too many unpleasant associations for him."

"What I'm getting at, though," Dr. Vosbergh continued, "is — here, everything Dr. Sterling's been wanting is ready to happen. And he still hasn't withdrawn his resignation. I hear you're going to leave us, too."

"I've put it off," Ellen said. "I'm going to stay as long as Dr. Sterling's here."

"Well nobody's trying very hard to find

a replacement," Dr. Vosbergh scowled. "Frankly, I'm terribly disappointed in the doctor, and I've told him so. It's almost a slap in the face to the people who've stood by him all this time."

"Maybe he's had all he can take," Ellen said. "It's all very well for people to laud him, now that a number of youngsters owe their lives to him. Still . . . he was the same dedicated doctor all the time this town treated him like a . . . a criminal. That isn't easy to forget, Dr. Vosbergh. Maybe it's too late."

"When you stormed into that Board meeting," Dr. Vosbergh said, "I couldn't have agreed with you more. This town didn't deserve him. But we can all be wrong, can't we? And when we say we're sorry . . ."

Ellen found it difficult to look into the old doctor's eyes. "No one's come up to him yet and said, 'We accused you of a crime you didn't commit.'"

"He knows he can refer any . . . doubters to the sheriff," Dr.

Vosbergh argued. "No, no, I'm sorry. Dr. Sterling's walking out at a time when this hospital needs him more than ever. He was stubborn enough, sticking it out when a few people were risking their livelihoods to defend him. Leaving now . . . the way I see it, it's showing the grossest ingratitude to his friends. Especially Porter Hubbard."

★ ★ ★

Porter had been too busy since the accident for socialising. With the zeal of an evangelist, he had been taking advantage of Henry Barfield's chastened attitude, rallying a grateful populace behind its hero doctor.

Jerry Sterling had been busy, too — not only with the accident victims, but since the glowing editorial in the *Barfield Register*, with an increasing number of new patients, some of whom had been delaying medical attention for an unreasonably long time. He didn't ask them why they hadn't got hospital care sooner; most, if they were honest, would have told him they had disliked the idea of being hospitalised miles away from home, in Templeton.

As a result of the increased patient load, Ellen had barely spoken to Jerry, except in the line of duty. Conversely, he seemed exceptionally anxious to talk when Ellen came into his office with the release form for Dr. Vosbergh.

"Dr. Grath should be here to make his rounds shortly," Jerry said. He placed the printed sheet in a wire basket on his desk. "He'll sign our old complainer out then."

Ellen started for the door. "I hope it's soon. Dr. Vosbergh's champing at the bit."

"He'd better take it slow and easy," Jerry grumbled. "He gets too excited when . . . well, for example, when he wants to make a point."

"I just walked out on him before he worked himself into a tizzy," Ellen said, turning around in the doorway.

"For the record, Doctor, he was talking about you."

Jerry's muscles seemed to tense. "Oh?"

Ellen realised instantly that he was remembering the confidences she had overheard in Dr. Vosbergh's room. "It wasn't anything . . . personal. Just that he regrets your leaving. He said you owe it to . . . " Ellen sensed that mentioning Porter Hubbard's name might draw her deeper into an area that Jerry considered none of her business. She finished the sentence lamely: " . . . to patients who never doubted your integrity."

Surprisingly, Jerry said, "Can you spare a few minutes? I'd like to talk to you."

Ellen looked questioningly at the open door. "Do you want me to shut . . . "

"Please," Jerry said. "Come back and sit down."

Ellen closed the door and seated herself in a leather chair opposite Jerry's desk. Unaccountably, she found her breath constricted.

He appeared uneasy, too, drumming his fingers on the desk top and inhaling deeply before he said, "If you don't want to hear what I'm going to say, please stop me anywhere along the line and I'll understand. It's just that I've got to talk to someone about it. You happened to be unlucky enough to . . . to have heard something I can't . . . " Jerry sighed. "Something I can't handle alone."

For a moment, Ellen felt a brief resentment. When had he been completely alone to face his problems? Hadn't he seen others standing by him, believing in him? In her own case, wanting more than anything else to lift the terrible burden that had been imposed upon him? Perhaps Dr. Vosbergh had been right; Jerry either wasn't aware of, or he didn't appreciate, the efforts others had made on his behalf.

Perhaps the problem was too painful

to articulate. Jerry took a circuitous route: "It's ironic. I shouldn't be using a new shoulder to cry on, considering that I've lived here most of my life. I realise you aren't a stranger in town, but . . . I didn't know you until you came to work here. You didn't know me."

Ellen lowered her eyes. *I loved you ten years ago, I never stopped loving you. Why did you think I came back?* (Why couldn't she tell him this?)

"We've worked together," Jerry continued. "I flatter myself that you were convinced of my competence as a doctor. Though why you should have committed yourself in a belief in me as a . . . as a decent human being, I'll never understand. You — maybe I'm wrong. You seemed to have faith in my innocence before you heard Dr. Vosbergh — before you heard Sheriff Garvey repeat something he had simply assumed was understood by everyone in town. I'm not going to ask you why." Jerry managed an uncomfortable half-smile. "Woman's intuition, maybe."

Couldn't he see it? Ellen wondered. Had she camouflaged her love so successfully that it had never occured to him? And was this because he had closed his eyes to love, fearing its consequences in himself, blind to it in others?

"That's one of the reasons for imposing on you now," Jerry was saying. "That, and the more obvious reason that you were an unwitting listener to . . . something I can only discuss with a trusted friend. Apart from you, there's been only one other friend I could have talked to this way. And the thing that's eating out my insides concerns him."

Jerry got up from his chair, suddenly too agitated to sit still. "Do you remember what I said after we left Dr. Vosbergh's room? Do you know what I'm talking about? Night after night, wondering who it was that turned my life into a nightmare.

Someone was responsible. Someone probably living right here in Barfield. Someone who told my wife, 'Don't tell your husband. There's another doctor who . . .'" Jerry stopped abruptly, one fist beating a frustrated tattoo against the top of the small filing cabinet next to his desk. "The sheriff's department assumes it was an old alcoholic who commited suicide soon after . . . "

"I'd heard that," Ellen said. "They closed the case on that assumption."

"And the news was played down. I don't have to tell you who it was that didn't want the Barfield name dragged through the mud." Jerry returned to his chair and sank into it disconsolately. "Or, maybe Henry Barfield couldn't accept that theory. As driven as he was, maybe he preferred to think I was responsible. That's not what I'm trying to say. What's tearing me up is . . . remembering that I swore . . . somehow, some day . . . I swore I'd get my hands on whoever sent Naomi to . . . to a drunken butcher."

"And she referred to the man as 'Hubby'," Ellen said softly.

"Can you understand why I had to talk to someone about it? I can't think — I can't sleep! A flimsy word like that. It could have been misheard. Dr. Vosbergh might have remembered wrong. How can I walk up to a man who's done everything humanly possibly to convince people that I didn't kill my wife — walk up to him and say, 'It was you!' And, yet, I — in retrospect, I remember — the nonchalant way in which Naomi would suggest including 'Hubby' in all our plans. Reminding me that, after all, he was my best friend. Or — when I had to work late and we'd planned to go to a dinner party; 'Hubby' was always available to fill in. All so innocent and above board! And I was terribly in love with her — always so fond of him." Jerry rubbed a hand over his eyes. "I could be so wrong, Ellen. I know what it means to be accused when the accuser is wrong."

"You can't forget it, can you?" Ellen

asked. "You won't be able to live with yourself until you're sure."

"No," Jerry said. "If I'm wrong, even the suspicion — telling you all these ugly things — is unforgivable. I don't know. I'm obsessed with it now and I don't know a way to escape from it. To reward that kind of loyalty with . . . "

"We don't have cures for some of the worst diseases," Ellen said softly. "Jealousy. Suspicion. The need for revenge. You know, Jerry . . . " She cut her speech off, shocked by the sound of his name. "I'm sorry. I didn't mean to . . . well, inside the hospital, anyway, it's a breach of ethics . . . "

"I haven't been talking to you as a nurse," Jerry said. "Go on with what you were saying, Ellen."

Their eyes met for a fleeting instant, and inwardly Ellen cursed her inability to control the sudden shivering of her body, the quavering of her voice. "I was thinking of a night when the same suspicion haunted me. About my own brother." Ellen looked up to see the stunned expression on Jerry's face. "It's monstrous to be telling you this. But . . . Lorna Barfield said it. I've heard . . . "

"*There were others,*" Jerry said grimly. "There wasn't only one man. *But only one man let her die!*"

"Maybe you're never going to know who it was," Ellen told him. "I felt the way you do now. About David. I kept asking him questions. Sly questions; hatefully suspicious questions. And I know now that he would have broken wide open if my grilling had had any basis in fact. A fundamentally decent man who makes one horrible mistake goes through hell. David wasn't tormented by his conscience. Like most people — my mother, the other nurses here, sensitive people — he just found it uncomfortable to remember a tragic death. That was why he didn't want to go to that shoddy place where that abortionist made his contact. Why he didn't want to look at the place on the road where . . . "

"A fundamentally decent man," Jerry was repeating. Once again, just as he had looked far beyond Ellen after that 'deathbed confession' from Dr. Vosbergh, he was staring into space, talking absently as though to himself. "A man like that could struggle with his conscience only so long."

"You wouldn't have to accuse him," Ellen said. "Is that what you mean? If you took him to The Tumbleweed — if you parked for a moment at that place by the road . . . "

Jerry shook himself out of a dazed mood. "It's not a bold, infallible plan. If a man's innocent, it's only a . . . dirty scheme."

"If a man's innocent, it's more vicious to go on questioning him," Ellen said. "Isn't that what you're trying to resolve?"

Jerry's telephone rang. "I'm expecting a long-distance call and it might take some time," he said. The phone rang again as Ellen got up to leave the room. "We'll . . . talk again, Ellen. Thank you."

A lengthy, private long-distance call implied that Jerry had made contact with another hospital. Or, perhaps the call was from an applicant for the vacancy at Barfield. Depressed by both possibilities, Ellen was in the corridor when she learned that the call was not the one Jerry had been expecting.

"I know. I know," she heard Jerry saying. "I've been tied up, too, Porter. What about having dinner together tonight? I think I can get Vernon to relieve me." There was a brief pause, and then: "Yes, I was thinking of inviting her myself, Porter. Not for a victory celebration, though. More of a . . . farewell party."

13

MOM'S chef had outdone himself, and now, as they sat in one of the small upstairs dining rooms at the dinner house, Porter Hubbard was in an exceptionally jovial mood.

"Signatures? I'll swear everyone in Barfield who can lift a pen has signed the petitions, Jer. It's a mandate from the citizenry. What did I tell you? All we wanted was time."

"What we want," Jerry said with studied casualness, "is a change of scenery. No offence against your mother's place, Ellen, but it's been a long time since I had a look at the outside world. It's beautiful out. What say we take a drive?"

"Great," Porter agreed. "Maybe you'll be more rational with some fresh air in your lungs pardner."

Jerry's Buick had reached a spot on the outskirts of town where two highways intersected before Porter stopped his attempts at persuasion. "Let's run up and see how the Rock River dam's progressing. I haven't seen it yet, but I hear they've got all the framework up."

"Since that bus accident, I've lost some of my taste for mountain driving," Jerry said. He had already turned into the flat route towards Templeton.

Porter accepted the decision easily. "You'll get over that. It was a rainy night, remember." He smiled. "We're getting old, Jer. I remember when we used to take the high road up — in that hot rod of yours, remember? Tearing around in those grades . . . "

"You're remembering Naomi's sports car," Jerry corrected.

Mention of the name had a settling effect on all three of them. Seated between the two old friends, a man she loved and a man who had expressed his love for her, Ellen was aware of a fourth presence. *Naomi always drove fast. Laughed, and drove fast, the way she lived.*

They drove in silence for a few minutes, Jerry's tension communicating itself to Ellen. He's hating himself for this, she thought. He's wrong . . . he knows he's wrong and he's ashamed of what he's doing. She felt a wave of shame, too, for having implanted the idea in Jerry's mind.

"Something wrong?" Porter asked.

Jerry had slowed the car almost to a stop. He was forcing himself to look toward a clump of bushes at the roadside. "You know where we are, don't you, Porter?"

Pressed against Porter, Ellen felt his muscles tighten. "I can . . . guess. I didn't know the exact place."

Jerry turned from the wheel for a moment, fixing Porter with a searching scrutiny. "You didn't know, or you don't remember?"

"The paper never pinpointed the exact spot." Porter frowned. "You're getting morbid, Jerry. It's not good for you to dwell on ghosts. It's past. It's over. You've got to . . . "

"Forget it?" Jerry had propelled the car forward again. "Have *you* forgotten it, Porter?"

"Of course I haven't forgotten it!" Porter's irritation was hardly a clue to a troubled conscience. He was no more nervous than David had been under the same circumstances, and what he said made sense. "I don't expect you to dismiss it from your mind completely — especially not after what you've been through. I just think it's . . . something all of us wish had never happened. And going out of your way to resurrect bad memories isn't a healthy thing. Killing yourself with work isn't good, either, but it's better than digging up the past and brooding over it."

"I've never gone to the cemetery," Jerry said. If anything, he seemed to be more distressed than Porter. Ellen noticed that his hands trembled on the steering wheel. "I have a lot to forget."

"Sure, and you've been trying," Porter said. "Look, let's talk about something else. I wanted to tell you — I met with Henry and Dale Bannister today. Sort of an ad hoc budget committee. We'll still have to get Board approval, understand, but we came up with a plan for expanding the hospital services that you won't be able to resist, Jer. Listen to this . . . "

Porter was still painting a rosy picture of added hospital personnel, new equipment and the purchase of two more ambulances, as Jerry cut through the outskirts of Templeton and started on the circular route towards Barfield.

"I thought you were soured on mountain driving for a while," Porter observed.

"We'll just go up as far as The Tumbleweed and then we'll turn back," Jerry said.

Porter shrugged. "Nice view from up there."

"I thought we could stop in for a drink."

Ellen had the sensation of sitting between two electrically charged wires, though Porter's disapproval sounded calm and logical. "Why would you want to go there? It's got to have terrible associations for you, Jerry."

"Why?"

"You know why. What's come over you, boy? This was supposed to be a relaxing . . . "

"*Why* should it have terrible associations for me?" Jerry persisted.

"Because the sheriff told you why it should," Porter said sharply. "Look, if this is therapy, fine. If you've got to face it once and for all, I'll come up here with you and you can run it out of your system. Maybe it's something you should have done long ago, but I don't think it's fair to Ellen, to drag her through all this."

The sincerity of Porter's argument had a sobering effect on Jerry. "I suppose you're right," he conceded. If the colour of his face was any indication, he felt sick inside, convinced that he had demeaned an old friendship with a shabby trick. And here was Porter, so completely above cheap machinations that what Jerry was trying to do hadn't crossed his mind; his concern was for Jerry and for Ellen.

Ellen felt her own taut nerves relaxing. Jerry was satisfied. The poison of suspicion had been drained from him, probably leaving regret in its stead. A word misquoted, a name carelessly remembered; these were flimsy threads with which to strangle a loyal friend.

Jerry said nothing more about stopping in at The Tumbleweed. When he turned his Buick into the dusty grounds surrounding the tavern and the cabins, Ellen would have sworn that he intended to circle behind the main building and return to the highway. In the parking lot area behind The Tumbleweed, he slowed down to an almost complete stop. Ellen saw his reason; their passage was blocked by a wide, muddy rut, made impassable by the recent rains. But Porter had been looking out the window at his side, towards the peeling, hideously orange, green and Dutch-blue motel units. As the car stopped, he must have assumed that they were all to get out. He did so, moving swiftly for a man of his massive proportions, and Ellen expected him to hold the door open, offering to help her out of the car.

She heard Jerry say, "What're you doing?" He hadn't moved from the driver's seat. Ellen sat still beside him, seeing Porter move a few feet away from the open car door. Jerry sucked in a quick, strident breath.

Porter was standing like someone in a trance, his eyes open wide in a kind of uncomprehending horror, moving from the cabins to the back of the inn, and finally, with excruciating slowness, to Jerry. His voice, when he finally spoke, was barely more than a whimper. "I can't go in there, Jerry. I'm . . . I'm sick."

Jerry leaped out of the car, rushing to Porter's side. "Why are you sick,

Porter?" His hands had closed over the lapels of Porter's suit. "You were here before, weren't you? You brought Naomi here . . . "

"Once! Yes, once," Porter cried. "Jerry, I didn't know she'd come here to that quack. I didn't know what to do. When she told me about the baby, I nearly lost my mind, but I thought . . . she'll go to Vosbergh. He'll help her. And I wasn't sure . . . I couldn't believe I was responsible. For months, after I told her we couldn't see each other any more. I knew she was running around with every . . . "

Jerry's savage cry was timed with the swinging arc of his fist. "*You . . . swine!*" The blow smashed Porter's lips against his teeth, jerking his head backwards. He lost his footing, stumbling backwards, one of his feet slipping in the muddy ooze and throwing him to the ground.

"Don't! Please!" Ellen slipped out of the car, reaching out to restrain Jerry. He brushed her aside, diving at Porter's sprawling figure, pounding the agonised face with his fists insanely. His breath erupted from him in dry, animal sobs; he was releasing a full year of frustrations and angers, the reason for his torment crystallised in the object before him.

"Jerry . . . stop! Please don't . . . !"

Ellen's pleas were drowned out by the brutal sounds of assault. Helpless, she tried screaming for help, but the scream congealed in her throat. She was leaning over Jerry, trying to stop the wild thrusts of his arms, when suddenly he was still.

No match for Porter Hubbard, Jerry must have realised that his more powerful friend wasn't fighting back. Slowly, he drew back, leaving Porter lying in the muddy ditch. He was breathing hard, staring unbelievably at the blood trickling from Porter's mouth, as Ellen stepped forward to help Porter struggle to his feet.

"I didn't kill her," Porter was sobbing. He edged away from Ellen's support, staggering to lean against the front of the car, seemingly unaware of his bleeding mouth and the wet mud dripping from his clothes. "All evening . . . when you kept saying things that . . . told me you knew . . . I kept wanting to tell you. I tried to make it up to you. I couldn't. I . . . went through a hell worse than yours, Jerry. At least . . . you could live with yourself. But . . . I didn't take her to . . . "

Jerry leaped forward as Porter fell across the bonnet of the car, his head banging against the metal with a heavy thump. "Ellen . . . help me get him into the car."

They were struggling to get Porter's limp body into the back seat of the Buick when a man emerged from the rear door of The Tumbleweed. He wore a bartender's apron, badly soiled, and his swarthy face looked as though it had never been creased by a smile. Approaching the Buick, he yelled, "What's goin' on out here?"

"This man's been hurt," Jerry puffed. "I'm a doctor . . . we're giving him first aid and then we're taking him to the hospital."

Drawing nearer, the man's reptilian glance darted from Porter's battered face, to Ellen, and then to Jerry. "Friend of yours, Doc?"

"Yes," Jerry said. "Yes. A very good friend."

A wary recognition glinted in the man's eyes. He had seen Porter Hubbard before. Had he been present at the inquest, or did he remember Jerry from pictures in the *Barfield Register*? He didn't move to help Jerry and Ellen, and his interest seemed only superficial when he asked, "Your friend been hurt bad?"

Unlike Ellen, the owner of The Tumbleweed couldn't have understood the break in Jerry's voice as he replied. "Yes. Yes, he's been . . . very badly hurt."

14

THE man with the cobra eyes came into the conversation several weeks later, while Ellen was tidying the Barfield Hospital operating room after a routine tonsillectomy.

The operation had been performed on one of Dr. Grath's patients, and he had accompanied the little girl to Recovery, along with Miss Llewelyn, and another assisting nurse. Jerry Sterling lingered behind, and, as so often happened now when he and Ellen found themselves alone together, they found themselves discussing the subject that refused to die.

"If I hadn't been so stunned at the time," Jerry said, "I would have heard what Sheriff Garvey told me. That poker-faced barkeeper told him that he'd seen Naomi at his place a number of times. Never with the same man."

"You must have been too distraught to accept that at the time," Ellen suggested. "We all tend to reject the things we don't want to believe." She gathered up instruments from a Mayo stand and carried them to a steel sink in an adjoining room.

Jerry followed her, untying the green surgeon's mask he had pushed down around his chin earlier. "That's it. It was hushed up anyway, and after that I was so busy fighting for my own survival that I didn't think to check back with Garvey. I knew the witness hadn't named any names. He clammed up — probably afraid he'd lose his licence."

"That seems to be a chronic threat," Ellen murmured.

"My point is . . . if I *had* checked it out then, I would have learned one thing. Months after . . . my wife was seen at The Tumbleweed with . . . others, she came to the place alone. Two or three times. *Alone*."

"And contacted . . . "

"Her executioner." Jerry sighed. "I'm glad I believed that when Porter said it. I did, you know. I believed he didn't . . . "

"Don't talk about Porter any more," Ellen said. "You'll start tormenting yourself with the fact that he's gone."

Jerry trailed behind Ellen again as she gathered up the linens from the operating table and deposited them in a hamper. "He needed help, Ellen. There isn't a psychiatrist in town. I gave him the name of a former classmate of mine — practises in San Francisco."

"That's a long way from Barfield."

"The way Porter loved this town, anyplace would have been far away. He couldn't stay here, though. I knew it couldn't ever be the same between us, but I argued with him. No one knows the truth except you and me." Jerry's fingers thumped against the autoclave. "You and I and — maybe a barkeeper who makes it a practice to keep his mouth shut."

"I would have told him that, too,"

Ellen said. "Except that he wouldn't see me."

"He said he couldn't look anyone here in the face again. Even telling him that running away would arouse suspicions where none exist — even that didn't help. Porter kept repeating, '*We can't both live in this town, Jerry. I meant it when I said you were needed here.*'"

But how did a man get well — what psychiatrist could help Porter rid himself of crushing guilt in a strange place, uprooted from his friends, separated from a business that represented his income, torn from the social and civic activities around which his life revolved?"

Ellen swiped at the tears with the back of her wrist. "Will he come back, do you think?"

"I don't know," Jerry said quietly. "If he does, he'll learn what I'm learning."

Ellen looked up, letting her dark eyes ask the question.

"The ghost is gone." Jerry was silent

for a moment, and when he spoke again he spoke with the renewed strength of a man who has put the past behind him. "This time — she isn't coming back."

★ ★ ★

But the ghost of Porter Hubbard's tragedy came back to haunt them. Late that afternoon, Mr. and Mrs. Eliot, representing a citizens' committee, came to Jerry Sterling's office to lay a thick sheaf of papers on his desk.

Ellen was present when they came, hearing Joan Eliot's soft-spoken mother say, "We would have had these petitions here a week ago, Dr. Sterling. But maybe you know our committee chairman was called out of town suddenly. Things never move as efficiently in this town without Mr. Hubbard."

After that, Mr. Eliot delivered a brief, rather stilted speech on behalf of the committee, and then they were gone.

195

Jerry didn't pick up the papers on his desk. Except for the first page, on which was typewritten a statement beginning, "*Whereas, we the citizens of Barfield recognise our need for a well-equipped and well-staffed hospital . . .* " — except for this, and the dozen odd 'whereases' paying tribute to Jerry Sterling that followed, the many sheets of paper consisted only of signatures.

Jerry leaned over his desk, thumbing through the pages. "Morgan. Levine. Kasanjin. There seems to be an absence of Whitakers."

"We're there," Ellen told him. "Page fourteen was posted at my mother's dinner place. The three of us signed it first."

Jerry didn't take time to verify the fact. He turned from his desk quickly, his arms reaching out to encircle Ellen like those of a ' desert-parched man reaching for an oasis, "Ellen . . . "

She clung to him, knowing instinctively that he was silent because there was too much to say. He had been alone too long, loveless too long. He had thought himself alone when he was not alone, unloved when he was not unloved. Where were there words to express this tangle of emotions? Where, for that matter, could Ellen find the words with which to reply?

Knowing this, Jerry drew her closer, planting his lips against Ellen's in a long, hungry kiss. And knowing it, too, Ellen returned the kiss. Words would come later. Plans for the future, admissions that for Ellen this was not a new love, promises to love and to honour . . . all these could wait, because, between them now, mere words were assumed.

They touched upon the words later, in the minutes before a ringing telephone summoned them to the delivery room. From the window of Jerry's office they looked out at the town. David's 'good people' lived here, making mistakes, hurting each other, helping each other and, more often each day, coming to

Barfield Hospital because they needed to be helped.

Looking out at the black and white signboard that fronted the church, Ellen noticed that the letters had not been changed since the day after the bus accident. JUDGE NOT, LEST YE BE JUDGED, the letters read.

Jerry's arms tightened around her. "It's not a bad town," he said.

Ellen had already told him that her letter to the Chicago hospital sat on her dresser at home, unmailed.

"It's not a bad town," Jerry repeated. "To work in, to raise a family in, to . . . " He leaned down to kiss Ellen once more. "People and towns are a lot alike. We seem to learn all our lessons the hard way."

"But people *do* come back here," Ellen said, just before the telephone rang. "*You* went away and came back. I did."

Jerry didn't mention the name that hung between them. As he picked up the receiver to answer the call from an anxious nurse in OB, he said, "When a guy really loves a place, it shouldn't take a signed petition. A little understanding — a little encouragement . . . "

"And a friend who's big enough to forgive?"

Jerry nodded slowly at Ellen. "Some day, like all of us, he'll come back home."

THE END

WITH SOMEBODY ELSE
Theresa Charles

Rosamond sets off for Cornwall with Hugo to meet his family, blissfully unaware of the shocks in store for her.

A SUMMER FOR STRANGERS
Claire Hamilton

Because she had lost her job, her flat and she had no money, Tabitha agreed to pose as Adam's future wife although she believed the scheme to be deceitful and cruel.

VILLA OF SINGING WATER
Angela Petron

The disquieting incidents that occurred at the Vatican and the Colosseum did not trouble Jan at first, but then they became increasingly unpleasant and alarming.

DOCTOR NAPIER'S NURSE
Pauline Ash

When cousins Midge and Derry are entered as probationer nurses on the same day but at different hospitals they agree to exchange identities.

A GIRL LIKE JULIE
Louise Ellis

Caroline absolutely adored Hugh Barrington, but then Julie Crane came into their lives. Julie was the kind of girl who attracts men without even trying.

COUNTRY DOCTOR
Paula Lindsay

When Evan Richmond bought a practice in a remote country village he did not realise that a casual encounter would lead to the loss of his heart.